Quicksand

Dyllan J. Erikson

Copyright © 2017 Dyllan Erikson

ISBN-13: 978-1974610815
ISBN-10: 1974610810

All rights reserved. This book or parts thereof may not be reproduced in any form, stored in any retrieval system, or transmitted in any form by any means—electronic, mechanical, photocopy, recording, or otherwise—without prior written permission of the publisher, except as provided by United States of America copyright law.

Formatting by Elaine York, Allusion Graphics
Publishing & Book Formatting, www.allusiongraphics.com

Quicksand

Please be advised, there are scenes of potentially distressing material surrounding PTSD in this book.

Prologue

~Elli~

The silhouette of his back is breathtaking, everything I adore about my husband in a single dark shadow. With his position facing away from me he doesn't see the tears that pour from my eyes. The skin on my cheeks feels hot and raw with every tear that silently tracks over them. My bright blue eyes feel dull and achy, no doubt swollen and red. My husband chooses to turn a blind eye to my tears, my anguish and desperation. Just as his back is turned now, he has left me completely alone in our relationship. A figurative shun, a literal hell. I know he doesn't know me anymore, and I think what hurts the most is that I no longer know him either.

"Garrett, baby please just talk to me. I can help you. I know I can," my plea whispering across my lips, falling on deaf ears. More tears threatening to blur my vision, only serving to irritate me. Each drop of water making me feel increasingly vulnerable and weak.

He doesn't turn toward me, my words just hanging in the air between us, he just shakes his head slowly from side to side with the utmost control. This robotic person in front of me is not the man I married. This thing in front of me isn't my best friend, isn't the one I vowed to love until death do us part. My heart constricts painfully while I realize some type of death has already parted us.

"G," I pause, walking toward him. "Please look at me." To anyone else, the anguish in my voice would be heart breaking, but not to him. He likely doesn't even recognize it being there at all. I watch his shoulders tense at the use of my nickname for him. Ever so deliberately he turns my way, each small movement making me feel hopeful that he'll come to me. Each achingly slow inch making me want to believe he might look at me with love again and not this distant coldness that's become our new normal.

He completes the turn, and I'm left feeling worse than when I couldn't see his face at all. I see now that I was foolish to hope, foolish to think he would look at me with anything more than contempt. What I wasn't the slightest bit prepared for was the look of hatred, so cold, so sharp that I feel it carving my heart out. What I see in those grey eyes breaks what's left of my heart, the pieces shattering on the floor, mimicking shards of broken glass.

"What do you want from me, Elli?" he growls in a tone that makes the hair on the back of my neck stand on end. I want to answer him but it's too hard now. I wanted him to face me and talk to me like we aren't two strangers living in the same space. But I can't. I physically can't. The way he said my name wasn't loving, wasn't the way a husband should ever say his wife's name. It sounded like a curse, something you spit out quickly because if you don't, it'll leave a bad taste in your mouth. My silence must piss him off, his back tensing further. But then again, everything I do lately pisses him off.

"ANSWER ME ELLI AVERY, WHAT DO YOU WANT FROM ME?" His voice is a shotgun to my heart, filling my chest with lead bullets that leave me open and bleeding. He never talks to me like this, he never yells at me. Who is this man? I wrap my arms around my middle, hoping that if I squeeze myself hard enough I won't fall apart right there in our bedroom.

I hiccup, "I just, I just want to help you." The tears clog my throat, they blind me and blur the image of Garrett in front of me, distorting him so I can no longer see the man I love. Was he even here to begin with? My rushing tears reveal a shadowy version of the monster he's become. I hear his frustrated breath turn from a sigh to a curse and realize I don't know how to live like this anymore. I look down at my feet, clutching my sides so hard that my fingers ache, the pieces of me slipping through my embrace. His footfalls come closer and it frightens me. I shouldn't be afraid of him. I wouldn't have been before, but it's so different now. I sense his presence before I physically feel his touch. His hands brush against my arms so tenderly, such a contrast to how he was just treating me, that I flinch He runs them up to my neck where he uses the pads of his thumbs to stroke my throat, something he knows used to soothe me while also setting me on fire. His hands on me, his fingers caressing me so gently, it's too much and I feel myself breaking further. I don't know how to handle what's happening right now, hot and cold, back and forth. He leans down pressing his lips against my temple and I completely lose it. The first sob comes out as a hiccup and I let myself go from there, feeling every ounce of hurt coming from a dark place within. Just the simplicity of his touch unravels every single piece of me.

"I'm so sorry, baby, I don't know what's happening to me," he whispers against my hair, "and that's why you can't help me. I...don't even know how to help me." His voice slices through me the way he sounds so raw, so broken, so desperate to let me in while not knowing how. He pulls me hard to his chest and I can barely breathe, his scent surrounds me, comforting me while simultaneously terrifying me. What if we can't get through this? What if he pushes me so far away I never get him back? I wrap my small arms around him and hold on for dear life, feeling like this might be the last time he ever holds me this close.

"Don't cry, baby, I'm sorry, I'm so sorry," he whimpers into my hair, his lips peppering kisses over and over. I know in my heart he isn't okay. I know in my heart that my husband is drifting away from me bit by bit and it's killing me. It's killing us. The war inside me is so loud that it drowns out his apologies, they become background noise instead of something tangible I can forgive. So, I do the only thing I can in this moment and hold him close, unable to even think, even hope, even breathe.

He moves us to lie down on the bed, me curling up into his side with his strong arms locked around me. He acts as if I'm the one trying to leave him when it's the other way around. I force my mind to shut down and focus only on memorizing his touch the way his muscled arms hold me tight into his side. The way his breathing is evening out, a sick façade of calm washing over us. I can feel his shoulders slowly losing their familiar tension, his arms instead flexing around me, keeping me tucked into him, where I used to feel safe and wanted. I miss him. He's right next to me and I miss him as if he were still in Afghanistan. I let my body finally give into the exhaustion, feeding on his warmth and drift away. The ear resting over Garrett's heart listens to it beating steady and loud, lulling me into a false sense of security.

I'm having a dream so vivid about the day we married, that I could almost feel the sand on the beach, almost taste the salt in the air from the ocean when suddenly I'm flipped on my back with his hands around my throat. I scrape my nails against his forearms trying to get him to loosen his grip, using my whole body to try and buck him off of me. His eyes are so dark they're almost black and I know he isn't with me right now, he's back there, in Afghanistan, in combat. He presses me further into the mattress, this big man straddling me and slowly choking the life out of me. Pinpricks of tingling start from my fingertips and work slowly up my arms and I know I'm losing this battle. I struggle with everything I have, trying to get him to let up, but my arms feel foreign and heavy, the edges of my vision starting to blur. I barely feel my hands fall from where they were clawing at his arms, I barely recognize the fact that I can't see him anymore because my vision is so far gone. The only thought I can conjure is that my husband is killing me and he doesn't even realize he's doing it. I let myself give in to it, feeling almost that if I give up now I don't have to hurt anymore, I don't have to pretend. My body starts shutting itself down, the lack of oxygen finally becoming too much for it to take. As I start to drift away from life and a warm light beckons to me from a distance, the air returns. It's so strange that at first, I forget how to take it in. I start coughing and sputtering, taking in a big lungful of air and feeling my body come crashing back to this reality. This moment where I almost died at the hands of the man who claims to love me. I take in deep breath after deep breath and run my fingers gingerly over the welts his hands left on my throat. It hurts, but not nearly as much as my heart does. .

I can barely see him from where he's hiding in the shadows of our room but I hear him over my desperate gasping, his voice coming out low and broken, "I'm sorry, baby, I'm so sorry."

Chapter 1

~Elli~

To: usmcraider1@gmail.com
From: norwegianbeauty@gmail.com
Subject: For Whatever Reason I am Writing You.

Dear Usmcraider1,

I'm not really sure what to start off with...
But, I guess I'll take a shot at it.
My name is Elli, pronounced Ellie – it's Norwegian. I live in a small two story with just me myself and I. Oh, I do have a dog though. Right now it's just the two of us. We used to be three but now we're just two.

...what am I doing? This is stupid, I don't even really know why I'm writing to you. I have no idea who you are or how this is supposed to help me. This is supposed to help me get better.

So far I'm just spouting off random details about myself and it makes it seem like I want this to be personal, which this is just... not supposed to be.

This is me attempting to follow guidance and advice and make myself feel "better," make myself get over...him.

Well you know what usmcraider1? I don't need to do that.

I am just fine feeling bitter and empty. Bitter is such a rancid word for what I am, but it's what they all call me.

They look at me walking around with a blank expression and shake their heads, I'm the girl with the dead husband. I am the girl whose fire went out when he died. I am the outsider, the one who doesn't try to be normal anymore.

But you know what? I don't give one single fuck about it, about them.

They didn't bury the love of their life, they didn't get handed that rigidly folded American flag. They don't hear a noise and think it's their dead husband coming in the front door or moving around the kitchen.

They don't live with a black hole flexing and gaping inside them.

They can't comprehend my pain, the anguish that eats at me day after day.

They don't know what it's like to not have him here with me.

Not that this has anything to do with you, this has to do with the advice I am being stupid enough to follow.

My best friend, Jen, said reach out to someone who knows what Garrett went through. Reach out to someone who knows what a soldier feels like.

But let me ask you something.

Do you know what a Veteran's widow feels like?

Do you know what it's like for that Veteran's widow to go on living impossibly day after day with the knowledge their husband didn't want to exist in this world anymore?

Why am I even asking you this?

You're an absolute stranger, I don't know you, you don't know me... but if I erased it now I probably wouldn't write anything else.

Whatever. I wrote it all out anyway.

I hope all is well as it can be wherever you are.

Stay safe if that's an option...

-The Veteran's Widow

My eyes itch, begging me to close them and let them rest but I just can't.

I click send and shut my MacBook down.

What did I just do? When Jen told me about a pen pal program that connects you with a solider overseas I didn't want anything to do with it. Her rationale was that talking to someone who is experiencing living and fighting in the war would be able to give me some insight into why my husband came home damaged. She used Google to find a forum where soldiers volunteer their email addresses and people around the world can write to them. Jen chose one email address and pled her case with me. I truly wanted to deny her, most days I don't want to talk to anyone let alone someone that could potentially remind me of the husband I lost. But in the end, it made sense, this is my last resort to try and move on from this.

Really, what have I to lose?

Nothing, because I've already lost that, everything.

Worst case scenario, usmcraider1 trashes the message and I go on being the "bitter" bitch that everyone knows me as.

No harm, no foul right?

Well, really lots of harm no foul.

I've been aware of just how damaged I am for a long time.

I'm coming to realize, after all the time that's passed that's probably the only thing I can be. Losing my husband to suicide has been without a doubt the most horrific event in my life. It has changed every fundamental part of me and I fear I'll never be able to recover.

I lean back into the pillows behind me and let the hurt seep in once again.

God, when will I be okay?

It's been two years.

730 days.

Two impossible years since Garrett died.

I know better by now then to let myself think about him, but nonetheless, I let the memories consume me and bring me back to ground zero again.

Now, I am no longer the bright-eyed Scandinavian girl on the arm of my ruggedly handsome husband.

Nope, not me.

Now I fully resemble the last little stub of a candle. The one where the stick has burned down to nothing and the remains are channels of melted wax down the sides of a table.

My flame has been suffocated.

During the day I've learned how to keep the pain at bay, I try to avoid feeling any kind of emotion. It's easier to turn it all off than to struggle with filtering them. If I become a robot, going through the motions and ignore feeling anything I can stay safe and guarded from the hurt.

At night is when it becomes unbearable. I can't sleep because, like some sick clockwork when I close my eyes and let the silence come at me, I relive the scene all over again.

Blood, the metallic tang assaulting my nose.

The rich color of it almost black it's so concentrated.

His bare feet, his favorite cargo shorts.

So much blood. So much heartache.

I should move, shouldn't I?

I should run away, find some way to start over.

But how do you start over when your life ended along with his?

I suppose I can just keep breathing even if it feels forced and horrible.

I roll over, pulling his blanket over my shoulders and curl up. If I curl tight enough maybe the shards of my broken heart won't escape through my chest.

I know I'll see him in my dreams, I can only pray that I see him as he was before that day.

The day that ended two lives, my husband's literally and mine psychologically. The day that is seared so deeply in my mind I wonder if I'll ever escape it.

Chapter 2

~Raiden~

"Get up Raid, too fucking early to be dealing with this shit, man." Weston kicks my cot jostling me out of an uncomfortable sleep.

"Yeah, man, I feel it." I sit up, swinging my legs over the side to slip on my boots, feeling the grit of sand on my tongue. I'll never get used to the taste of sand, no matter what you do it always ends up right there, grinding between your teeth.

I take my time lacing up my boots, wondering if when I'm stateside again, it'll go away or if it'll be with me forever. The sand like a memory you can't shake, this place will stay with me. Too many brothers have fallen. Too many live with those memories you can't avoid from battle, so suffocating that you can practically see it clawing at them from the inside. No one knows how it feels but us. Those of us out in the deep shit, out there fighting and getting that blood on our hands and having to wash it away knowing it came from either the enemy or your best friend.

"Yo, Raiden you coming or what? I don't have all day to wait on your ass!" I hear Weston yell from outside the tent. Impatient as ever, but my best friend no matter what.

"Yeah man, I'm coming just let me get my head on first!" I shout back, shaking my head. Always riding my ass that one, but he's a good guy. I respect him and he respects me, we get some good banter going, have to keep things light or this place will swallow you whole and spit out nothing but your bones. Swatting open the flaps of our tent I make my way to the mess hall. A little food, a little coffee and I will be at least halfway functioning.

"Hey Michaels, it's your turn to dick around on the computer before we head out for the day." Gage – one of my platoon brothers- nudges me in the shoulder, a twinkle in his eye, like I'm gonna spend my time with the comm jerking it like he does. No thank you. Not my style. I'd rather have the real thing wrapped around me, not some cyber chick.

"Thanks, man, gonna head over now then." I grab my coffee and drain it in two gulps, it's shit, but at least it's something to get me going – you learn quickly in the desert that you take what you can get and shut up about it. I stomp over and into the comm tent, my boots kicking up dust. I grab the stool that's entirely too small for my big frame and start up the computer. It's a wonder this thing even works, like I said before - the sand gets everywhere.

Clicking open my email, I see the usual. Only a couple spam messages, one from my mom and one I don't recognize. Huh. Norwegianbeauty? I raise my eyebrows confused as all hell. Sounds like a sex offer site and I will not be buying that shit. I go to move it into the trash but stop when I read the subject line, "For Whatever Reason I am Writing You." That doesn't sound like a sex for hire site.

> *"Hi,*
> *I'm not really sure what to start off with... Well, I guess I'll take a shot at it.*
> *My name is Elli, pronounced Ellie."*

That's different, why is some chick named Elli emailing me? Reading on, my hands tighten into fists on the desk on either side of the computer. This girl... this woman sounds wounded, she sounds screwed up to be perfectly honest. What would she get out of writing me? *"They said to reach out to someone who knows what Garrett went through. Reach out to someone who knows what a soldier feels like."*

This really doesn't sound good. *"With the knowledge their husband didn't want to exist with her in this world anymore? Why am I asking you this...?"* And then she tore my heart right out of my chest with how she signed it.... "The Veteran's Widow."

Fuck me running. I don't know if I've ever read anything like that.. Made me feel like her whole situation is now my problem is what it did. I look down, realizing my knuckles are turning white with how clenched they are. Her husband killed himself. It sounds like PTSD, and the thought of PTSD taking another soldier nearly sends me into a blind rage. When a soldier comes home they should have the help they need, the help they deserve, this shit just shouldn't happen!

I can't even reply to her right now, or if I can at all, it's just hitting a little too close to home. I shut the computer down and use my rage to propel me out of the tent with The Veteran's Widow on my mind and already a fair amount of sand in my boots.

Chapter 3

~Elli~

I open my eyes and I see the stars. Not the sky, just the old cheap plastic glow in the dark stars on my ceiling that dim with every passing moment. I feel at times those poor fading stars are a metaphor for me, slowly losing their light, only tethered to this world by a small sticky part that just refuses to unstick.

I grunt, I should probably get up. I roll over to face my fur baby and rub Dahlia behind her bat-like ears. My furry partner in crime is one of the only things truly keeping me in this world. My parents would probably miss me...and Jen of course. What it really comes down to is that I'm just not that desperate yet. I know my light is dimmed and trying to leave me but something about inflicting the pain I feel because of Garrett on my family and best friend just feels too cruel.

I drag myself out of bed and move toward the hallway, hearing Dahlia flop off the bed. The sound of her pads slapping the floor follows me through the house to the kitchen where she knows there is food to be had. Dahlia was my birthday present a year before Garrett died, he surprised me with a beautiful and fierce German Shepard puppy that had my heart from the instant I laid eyes on her. We absolutely fell in love with each other, and the bond has only strengthened now that it's just us two.

I lean my hip up against the counter watching her hastily scarf her food and breathe deep, searching for the strength that I know is there to make it through another day. From beside me on the counter, my phone beeps with a message alert. Jen, my best friend in the world. Ugh, I wish that pain in my ass would be a pain in my ass another day, not today, I just don't have the energy for her. I swipe up my phone and read, "Hey girl, spa day this weekend my treat, okay? Don't you even try to bail; I will kick your sexy little ass clear to next Sunday."

I chuckle, she's pushy and blunt but even feeling as empty as I do, I can't not smile at her efforts. I tap out a reply and try at least a little to sound like I care if I have a spa day or not. To be honest, I stopped giving a shit about pampering myself. I can't remember the last time I paid any mention to my appearance. I just don't really try anymore. I just don't see the point.

I look across the kitchen into the living room where I can see myself in my full-length mirror. I wasn't able to keep food down for a few months after I found Garrett so my normally plump curves have deflated a bit into a toned but smaller version of myself. My eyes cast up to my blonde hair that has lost its shine but grown to fall just under my shoulder blades. My eyes, those are what bother me the most. Though they are an arctic blue, they just seem...lifeless. They roll at the thought, I know firsthand what lifeless eyes look like- how morbid- and... mine only have a pinch more life in them than that.

I look away from the mirror and try my best to clear my thoughts. A blank slate for a new day, anything is possible and all that jazz. I shuffle to the back door to let Dahlia out now that she's done scarfing her food, then sit back on a stool at the counter and run my fingers over my face. It's a nasty little habit I've formed, having my face hidden makes me feel safe, then maybe people won't notice me and I can stay in my hurt bubble and mope. I hear the telltale alert of my phone again, but when I go to check it I notice instead of my adorable yet annoying best friend it's an email...

To: Norwegianbeauty@gmail.com
From: usmcraider1@gmail.com
Subject: Sand

Hey Elli,

I don't really know where to start after reading all that.
But I guess I can tell you my name is Raiden. I am a soldier in the United States Marines, stationed near

Baghdad Iraq. It is a hot fucking disaster over here and if I had it my way I would be on a beach enjoying the only sand that I don't loathe with the ocean coming right up to my chair.

You like the beach, Elli? I used to go all the time when I was stateside, there's nothing like it.

What's your dog's name? What breed? I guess I'm askin' you these questions to get your mind off of everything for a minute. Because honestly, all I could picture while reading your email was a broken woman. A broken woman spreading her cracked and bleeding pieces out on a table and poking at them.

Don't. If there is anything I can say is, don't poke at the pieces, Elli, they'll just cut you deeper.

This is my third tour in this hell hole, and you said be safe if it's an option…Sometimes it is, sometimes it isn't but I have a damn good group of men around me and I do what I gotta do and come back to base.

I don't know how you feel, Veteran's Widow, but I know what it feels like to lose someone, to walk into it, see it firsthand… That's something I wish you wouldn't have gone through; I wouldn't wish it on anyone. But I know. I hope that helps because it's all I can offer. You said you were "stupidly" following advice in writing to me. Well, Elli, I'm glad you did…

-Raiden

My lungs are burning with the breath I didn't realize I was holding in. My eyes finish trailing over his name, *Raiden*. The name sounds so masculine to me, so strong and noble. I let my eyes close slowly and try to regain some kind of grip on myself. I haven't talked to a man in two years, save for my dad and that's few and far between. My phone feels like lead in my hand, the weight of his words taking away some of the weight that was sitting on my chest. I take my palm and rub it against my sternum, feeling how hot my skin is under the thin T-shirt I'm wearing.

I hear what I imagine his voice is, strong and deep, whispering to me, *"Don't poke at the pieces Elli, they'll just cut you deeper."*

Is that what I've been doing? Laying it all out there and forcing myself through a personal hell comparable to the real thing?

Sick self-torture?

Would it be so bad to just let myself move on?

Would it help?

My phone still sits heavy in my hand, Raiden's words still there on the screen, giving me strength I didn't know I had.

What is happening right now? I lock the screen and set it gently on my tile countertop, breathing in and out, letting in everything I try not to let myself feel. What is it about his reply that is making me want to open up? Basic human interaction with someone who doesn't know me, and doesn't know my story is refreshing. It's almost thrilling to be able to talk to someone and have them not pity me, he made me think about other things than my crushing guilt and sadness. Do I feel hopeful? Do I feel better? Will this email actually help me and now Jen will never drop it? Who knows. Sitting there and thinking it over, I feel some of those broken and cracked pieces inside me shift back, just a fraction, out of my heart as a smile ghosts my lips.

    What a way to start my day.

Chapter 4

~Raiden~

Sitting back on the stool after having just written what I hoped to be a reassuring email, I angrily scrub my hands down my face.

How can this woman have gone through something I can only imagine as terribly tragic? She didn't go into detail about what this Garrett did or what she walked in on but it clearly had horrific stamped all over it.

Ding.

I peek through my fingers at the sound of this ancient computer and see an email from Elli. She already emailed me back, right after I sent my reply. My pulse thunders through my ears, I have absolutely no idea what to expect here, but I can barely open it fast enough.

To: usmcraider1@gmail.com
From: norwegianbeauty@gmail.com
Subject: The Beach

Raiden,

I won't say thank you just yet because the pain I deal with every day is unimaginable. But reading your words of comfort and support coming from someone I haven't met...meant more to me than anything has in a long time.

I do like the beach and I do love the sand. Though I can safely assume this sand I love is different than the sand you're surrounded by. Which is why you said you loathe it, I'm assuming again that the sand in Iraq is much different than in the U.S.

I feel selfish writing you because now that I know your situation, I realize I truly have more to be thankful for than I am, even if I haven't been appreciating it

Why three tours? Voluntary? Garrett only did... you know what? I can't, not yet. I'm not going to talk about him, not even going to mention him again.

Tell me about what made your days on the beach so special? I need something to distract me from.... from feeling like I'm drowning.

My German Shepard is a two-year-old spoiled brat. Her name is Dahlia because dahlias are my favorite flower. Interesting I know. Some Marine in Iraq is getting told about favorite flowers, thrilling I'm sure, ha.

Stay safe,

-Elli

I read the email for the fifth time listening to my heart pound erratically in my ears. She responded... She said my words meant something to her, that they helped her somehow.

I can't remember the last time I felt like this, happy to help someone who isn't one of my brothers. Happy to help some woman I don't know from Eve.

I wonder what she looks like. I let my eyes drift closed, trying to imagine what Elli looks like. Something about the sarcastic, funny comment about me learning her favorite flower makes me think she's intelligent and witty. I bet she's fucking stunning, with a personality like that. It's messed up I guess but I have a feeling this wounded beauty is just that, a beauty.

"Michaels, where are you!?" Roused from my thoughts, I hear Weston shouting somewhere close to the comm tent. I close the computer and for the second time in not so many days, walk out into the hot air with thoughts of the Veteran's Widow on my mind and today the sand in my boots doesn't bother me as much.

Chapter 6

~Elli~

"Would you stop staring at me like that, Jen?" I playfully scowl in my best friend's direction while she just keeps staring at me. She's been like this since she picked me up twenty minutes ago, it is for sure pissing me off and not just because she is driving and not paying attention to the road. "Girlfriend, you are wearing makeup. You haven't worn even a little mascara in two whole years." She says this with an air of astonishment as if me wearing makeup is the biggest thing to ever happen.

I glance down at my hands clutching my phone like it's going to suddenly fly out of my hands and smirk just a little. "OH MY GOSH, E you're smiling!" I can almost feel the sonic blast from Jen's shrieking.

"OUCH Jennifer, what the hell is wrong with you!?" I giggle and shake my head, my hair falling in front of my eyes, another shield I put up when life feels a little too close. I like to pretend I live in a bubble of grief and hiding from life becoming normal again is just what I do. I guess it is kind of a big deal, she hasn't seen me make any effort to be anyone but a broken woman in what feels like forever. I really did try once, I used to love getting primped up and polished with her and hitting the clubs, dancing the night away.

I sit back for a bit and breathe deep, I feel good. For the first time in quite a while, I feel just a little more okay than I have been. Today I woke up and just felt like I could breathe a little deeper than I have in the past two years, not that I will ever get over the pain of losing Garrett, But, you know what? Mascara won't kill me.

I feel Jen side eyeing me again so I turn my full attention to her, twisting around in my seat. I level her gaze, knowing she has something to say and won't let me be until she gets it out.

"Honey, I don't know what happened to bring this on but...I am so glad it did." She gets watery at the last part and reaches out for my hand, which of course I take in my own because I didn't want her to cry because of me.

"Jen, you are my best friend and I know I haven't been here," gesturing around me, "in two years, but I finally feel like making an effort again. ." I turn back forward and give her a glance seeing she is full on grinning at me. So I grin back. A week ago I wouldn't have even smirked and it feels amazing.

We spend hours at the spa, having massages, manicures and pedicures and Jen even talked me in to having a makeover done. Although that might have been the bottle of wine we went through. When she dropped me off at home I grabbed a beer from the fridge and settled into the couch. Garrett's favorite beer to be exact. I never liked it when he was alive but there's just something comforting about tasting something he loved. I let the rich deep flavor wash over my senses. It's almost like he's here with me again, a small way to connect with him.

The last year when he came off tour was.... devastating. He just no longer resembled the man I married, the man who would do anything for me and would die before ever hiding anything from me. No, he was a stranger that I shared a bed with and it tore me apart. Every. Single. Day.

I take another sip and lean my head back, my blonde hair spreading out across the back of the couch. How could I have not known something was seriously wrong? Was I blind?

No, shaking my head back and forth in pain and frustration. No, I knew something was off, I knew it when I looked into my husband's deep green eyes. I fucking knew it. But he wouldn't talk to me and every time I tried to bring up the tour, he would snap at me. My Garrett never snapped at me. He was loving and attentive, he was forthcoming and he absolutely worshipped me.

I don't know that it is fully my fault for what happened, or that I should be blaming myself but I don't honestly know how not to. He was my responsibility.

That's what happens in a marriage, you become each other's responsibility.

I slip into my memories, clutching the bottle tighter. *Let the hurt consume you, Elli, give in to it.* I let my memories burn me with the white-hot fire that is always right under the surface. I let myself see his face, his big bushy beard his smiling lips under it, his green eyes looking at me adoringly. I smile at that memory using one hand to rub my chest where my heart used to be, remembering how it felt to be looked at like I was truly the only thing on this Earth that made any sense.

But a darker memory follows, his eyes change, they stare at me blankly, his smile no longer fills me up but leaves me empty and alone. I see him the afternoon I left to go have a workout with Jen, I can see his eyes assess me but never truly see me.

Oh God, his eyes. Those eyes that were no longer for me, but lost in some invisible battle I wasn't allowed to fight with him.

Then I see myself, like I am an ethereal spirit floating above my body watching the scene unfold with curious eyes. I feel myself clutch the bottle so hard I fear it might break. I turn the key in the lock, a huge happy endorphin fueled smile on my face wanting to smother my hubby in kisses.

Elli, don't do it, don't go in there! Ethereal me reaches out so close to grabbing me and pulling me back away from the entry of our house, but I cross the threshold anyway and a scream like no one had ever heard ripped through my throat. It was as if I was dying right along with him in that moment. A piece of me did die, along with the bullet that ended my husband's existence.

Opening my eyes and taking the last of the beer in my mouth I steel myself. I need to tell someone. I need to tell someone how it felt to walk in on him... I need to finally get this off my chest.

Chapter 6

~Raiden~

Weston and I make our way back to our tent, after what can only be described as a good day. A good day in war isn't the same as *any* good day, it just means none of my buddies died and I thank God for that.

I take my helmet off and shake out my hair, sand, of course, flying everywhere. I need a damn shower. I'm in a foul mood despite having a good day here in this hot madness. I wasn't concentrating hard enough today on the shit at hand, instead I was thinking of what I could possibly say to Elli.

She doesn't need to be talking to me when my existence isn't guaranteed. She went through her husband's tours and she knows the drill, she knows the uncertainty that comes with being over here fighting what I hope is the good fight.

I grab my clean clothes and head to the showers. They're outside in the open but they get the job done, I don't mind it. Letting the frigid water wash over my dirty, tired body I sigh. When will I get this chick off my mind. I don't do the dating thing, when I'm stateside I hit the bars, I find a hot little piece to take back to my place and send her packing as soon as I'm done with her. Not that I'm disrespectful but she needs to know where she stands with me, I don't do relationships for the expressed reason of what Eli is going through.

Who knows what I'm gonna be like when I'm done, either dead or fucked up I'm sure. No woman needs to deal with that, take that burden that isn't hers to have. God, putting someone who seems as sweet as Elli through that would destroy me all the way on the other side if that's where I ended up. No way. I protect women from that and enjoy getting my dick wet in the process. Besides that, I haven't wanted to love anyone enough to want to be with them for an extended period. Like I said, when I bring a woman home they need to know where they stand and with me, they really don't.

I finish up showering, glad the dirt isn't caking my exhausted muscles anymore, and resolve to go into the comm tent and tell Elli to stop writing me. It's for her own good, I know it. Maybe even for my own good too. I boot up the computer and click my email, knowing this is the only way she can heal. I probably can't help her and I need to accept that. My eyes widen in surprise when I see an email from her waiting for me.

To: usmcraider1@gmail.com
From: norwegianbeauty@gmail.com
Subject: Garrett

Raiden,

I was drinking Garrett's favorite beer after a day I am surprised to say I loved, getting dolled up and pampered with my best friend. I sat there feeling melancholy, tasting one of my favorite tastes that remind me so much of my husband.

Then I let what happened wash over me. I know, really heavy stuff but honestly, I need to tell you. I need to stop feeling this burning, this searing feeling that consumes my entire soul, what's left of it anyway. I just feel that even after a few emails you're there listening to me. The anonymity of us helps, if you knew me, you would know I haven't spoken to anyone about this. Phew, okay here it is...

When Garrett came back from his last tour in Afghanistan he wasn't the man I married. He used to look at me like I was the only woman in the world, and he would do anything for me. He did do everything for me. But when he came back, it was like the light inside him had gone out. We were partners in crime, best friends and yet he was shutting me out as if I was a stranger.

When I tried to talk to him about it, he would either shut down or lash out at me. It finally got the point where he unknowingly choked me until I saw stars. I thought maybe if I tried to get him to open up, we would be able to get through it. But we didn't, he only distanced himself more. I wasn't going to give up though, that was never an option for me. I would rather have died.

The day it...happened... I spent the morning with him, laughing and carrying on like nothing was wrong... and Raiden, he smiled at me. When it happened, it was so stunning to me that I lost my breath and I could almost feel my heart healing. I thought this was going to be the beginnings of a breakthrough...but I was so wrong. It wasn't quite the radiant smile from before but it was progress! I honestly could have cried. Jen came and picked me up to go to the gym for some pole dancing class she thought would be fun. When we came back I was on an absolute high so happy to come home to him, for once I was hopeful we could get back to who we were.

I walked in the door and there he was. In a pool of blood, the man I vowed to love until death do us part. Death had parted us.

In his hand was my pink little 9mm. He used the gun he had bought me as an anniversary present to shoot himself...shoot himself in the head. I don't remember what happened but I think the neighbors heard my screaming. Jen later told me that I blacked out, getting on my knees and holding his ruined head in my arms and screaming like I was the one dying. She truly thought I would die right along side him.

She said I was head to toe covered in his blood. When the police and the paramedics arrived, Jen have to physically drag me out of my house, our house.

I don't truly remember anything until after the funeral. I was in a fucking haze, a shredding debilitating haze. I do remember being handed that flag, though. That fucking stupid flag and having my husband's superiors give me their condolences. These men who sent my husband into battle, only to have it ultimately destroy him. Garrett was into something deep, something I wasn't ever allowed to know about, he was a Navy SEAL.

I know this all is a lot to take in and if you don't email me back, I would understand. Because Raiden, just writing this has helped me in ways you could never understand. I know it isn't easy to be safe over there, but promise me you'll try. You have given me so much in just a few emails that I could honestly never repay you. Thank you, Raiden. Thank you for giving me the strength to get this out. Thank you.

Stay safe,

-Elli

I drop my face in my hands and exhale what feels like knives. God, Elli. How could this woman have gone through that and not died from the anguish?

I look down at the instant message box in the corner of my email screen, thinking. I open it and click on Norwegianbeauty, my heart starting to race and my palms getting sweaty.

usmcraider1: **Elli?**

Radio silence.

It was a long shot but I needed to try to communicate better with her, be able to reach out in something more personal than an email. Especially after handing me all her sorrow on a silver platter and then giving me a way out.

Before, even a couple of hours ago, I might have taken it. Keep her safe from feeling like this ever again. After that confession, after showing me all her broken pieces I can't leave her alone. I just can't. Something took over me as I read her words, her hurt becoming my own.

I don't even know what she looks like, but I know I need to try to shield her from this pain, take it on, and give her relief. I don't even know where she lives, what time it is where she is.

norwegianbeauty: **Raiden?**

My inhale is sharp, almost more of a gasp. I let Elli fill me up. I need this, I need to connect with her.

usmcraider1: **What time is it there? Wherever you are.**

Please God let it be a decent time where she is, I have to talk to her.

***norwegianbeauty*: It's 9 am here, and I live in California by the way. (:
Why?**

She lives in my home state...I take a beat, rubbing my hands on my sweats and type out the first thing that comes to mind.

***usmcraider1*: Give me your phone number.**

***norwegianbeauty*: What? why??**

Please, just do it. I know too much about you now, I can't just know you from a computer screen.

***usmcraider1*: Please Elli, just do it.**

Please Elli.... I hang my head hopeful she'll do it, but then again, she doesn't even know me. What if she doesn't want some jarhead in the desert calling her?

***norwegianbeauty*: (909)-455-7960...**

Yes! I snatch the global phone off the desk, my pulse pounding like a jackhammer in my ears. I dial, but before I punch in the last number I stop. *What am I doing?* What is going on with me that I feel like I need to soothe this poor woman.

What I thought this morning still stands, what if we get attached? With me she is stuck with no certainty, she has gone through way too much for me to mess up the life she could have, the promise of no more pain. I stare at the phone in my hands, I bore my gaze into it, needing a sign that this is what I'm supposed to do.

Ding.

***norwegianbeauty:* Raid? You there?**

Fuck me. She called me Raid, no one calls me Raid.

My dick stirs in my sweats and I realize this is what I have to do. Future be damned I need to hear her voice; I need to know her.

Jesus, I don't know what I need, I just know I need this. I dial. And I wait.

Chapter 7

~Elli~

I'm sitting on my bed, Dahlia at my feet curled up, snoring, and I'm trembling. I don't remember a time when I was this nervous. I feel like my whole body is a knot. One giant knot.

Raiden is going to call me. *Why would he want to do that?* My cheeks start to heat, thinking about hearing this man's voice. This man who listens to me and gives me strength when I feel too weak.

I sit there with my computer up, his IM's on display with my phone resting against my thigh.

I gave him my number because why not? I feel daring, like finally living for once. It has to be like eight pm over there in the desert, doesn't he need to unwind and sleep? I don't know what he even does over there, maybe I should ask. But maybe he can't tell me like Garrett couldn't. I let my mind wander waiting for him to IM back or call me, but for a solid five minutes, nothing happens.

I shoot him a quick "Raid? You there?" hoping like hell he didn't change his mind. I sigh, realizing maybe I've been lonelier than I let myself believe.

Just when I go to IM him again, my phone lights up and I startle nearly jumping a foot in the air. I can't stop staring at it like it's possessed, my hands clutching my chest feeling a heart attack coming on. It's a global cell call, Garrett used to use those to call me when he was on tour... I wait a couple rings, still uncertain at what I'm doing and concerned at my reaction to this in the first place. But, breathing in deep I click to answer.

I freeze. I can't breathe, the little breath I had escapes me and leaves no air behind. I can't think, I just take these weird little puffs of inhales that mimic breathing but in truth I am not fully functioning on the breathing thing. *Why am I so nervous?*

"Elli?" Oh, my God. His voice is strong and steady, deep with a sensual bass. So much better than I had imagined.

"H... Hi Raiden," I squeak out. I shake my head, mad that that's the first thing he's heard of me, this meek little voice. So, I try again, clutching the phone to my face like it's going to suddenly disappear.

"What made you call?" Better, I sounded more myself there.

"I don't know, something made me want to check on you after that email." *He's concerned about me?*

"Yeah, I mean I needed to tell someone and I had been drinking. So, it ended up coming out like that."

My voice softer, loving the fluttering feeling I get from hearing his voice.

I glance down at the IM's between us again. Interested in the feeling in my belly, something strange and long lost. Something not really bad but something I haven't felt in years. I listen to him breathe, thinking of things to say to someone halfway across the world that I've never met. But he beats me to it, surprising me.

"Elli, that is some shit you went through. It isn't my place to say and don't hate me for it, but I don't think he should've let it go down like that. Your house, your gun... it just shouldn't have happened. Now you'll see that in your dreams forever." He sounds pissed, and that does something to me. I don't know what I expected, maybe pity for the poor Veteran's Widow, not anger on my behalf. It's so refreshing.

"I understand what you mean, I wish it wouldn't have happened either. But I can't change the past...no matter how much it weighs on me." I swallow, feeling the familiar anguish of Garrett's death looming over me, threatening to take me under once more.

I don't want to feel like that when I have Raiden talking to me, I want to be strong. I want to be normal. For once just be a woman, on the phone with a man having a normal conversation.

"Hey Raiden? What time is it there? Isn't it nighttime? Aren't you what, like eleven hours ahead of me? Are you tired? Should I let you go so you can get some rest?" I hit him with twenty questions to take the focus off of me. His quiet chuckling makes my heart feel things.

I strain to hear it better because the connection started to get fuzzy then but I hear it then, loud and clear. That feeling comes back listening to his deep laughter, unfurling deep in my belly and telling me to enjoy this. I smile and type an IM while he's still laughing and lighting up some of the dark that is my world.

***norwegianbeauty:* I like your laugh, Raid.**

I shake my head at myself, what kind of thing is that to say?! It was innocent though, he has a great laugh, maybe he needed me to tell him. I don't know, I feel like a teenager talking to her crush for the first time. Which is strange because I didn't really think of myself as capable of having a crush this late in the game. This isn't going to change the fact I love my dead husband, I just... it was innocent. *I'm allowed to do this.*

He stops laughing and inhales sharply, filling my head with his voice as deep and rich as bourbon, the good stuff.

"I like that you make me laugh, Elli." My eyes close and a smile tugs at my lips, the feeling in my belly spreading. I roll to my side, sinking into my pillows and holding my phone close.

"Tell me about you, I don't really know you." I close my eyes waiting for his gorgeous voice to come through again.

"Well, I grew up in South Pasadena, it was just me and my mom, my dad died when I was little but he was a Marine, Special Ops, so that's kinda how this happened for me. My mom and I were and are to this day best friends. I went to the beach as much as I could, I love surfing and sailing."

He takes a breath and I just listen to him with my eyes closed, wishing I knew what he looked like, with a voice like that it can't be bad.

"I have done three voluntary tours in Iraq and haven't regretted it once. I love what I do but mostly I love being around my platoon. They're truly my brothers and I wouldn't be able to imagine my life without 'em."

He goes silent so I say, "I'm glad you have your brothers, I'm glad you have people who can look out for you." He stays silent, so I press on.

"I live in Long Beach, so I get to be on the beach whenever I want. Looks like we grew up only a little ways apart from each other." He lets out a breath and says exactly what was on my mind.

"And now we are thousands of miles apart."

How could he have known that's what I was thinking? He lives so close when he's home, would it be so bad to maybe meet him in person? Meet the man who has already started rewriting my future? I let out a small gasp, surprised at myself for thinking that. He truly has though. Just by listening to me and providing me an unbiased ear, someone removed from the situation, he's given me so much.

"When are you done with your deployment, Raid?" I say it softly, but I know he hears me because his breathing grows a little harsher. "I'm done in five months."

Okay, that isn't bad. He could come home in five months, five months isn't that long. That isn't even half a year. I let myself lift up with hope in meeting this stranger who seems to have a knack for making me smile, even if it's just to thank him in person for being a crutch when I truly needed it.

"And Elli?"

I breathe, becoming addicted to how he says my name, hard and soft at the same time.

"Yes, Raid?"

He practically whispers then, but I can hear it loud and clear because of how it affects me. "I love it when you call me Raid."

I let his words wash over me like a tidal wave of happiness, interested as hell at how good it felt to hear him say that.

I hear some background noise so when Raiden says, "Hey I have to get going, but I'll be try to get in touch with you soon, okay?" I'm not surprised but what I am surprised at is how disappointed I feel.

"Stay safe... Raid," I whisper, wishing he could stay on the line just a little longer.

He just breathes, "Elli," as if he were saying a prayer. Then the line goes silent and I mourn the loss of his voice, and the comfort I didn't realize I craved.

I roll onto my back looking up at the dimming glow in the dark stars that right now, look brighter to me than they have in two whole years.

Chapter 8

~Raiden~

I'm lying in my cot, staring up at the ceiling of the tent I call home out here in the desert and I can't sleep. I need to be up in a couple hours because we're going out on a mission. I need to be focused, I need to be alert, keep my brothers safe, bring us all back in one piece.

But every time I close my eyes, I can't think of anything but how Elli's voice made me feel. Made me feel like I would do anything to protect that voice, anything to keep her safe from harm. I don't honestly know that I'm comfortable with this feeling.

I get lost in my own thoughts listening to the wind rushing around outside, the weather oblivious to my moral dilemma and confusion about a woman. Not just any woman though, she's a survivor. A fighter, like me. She fights every day a fight she doesn't know if she's gonna win. Just like me.

I let out a frustrated breath and sit up. Swinging my feet off the bed, leaning my elbows on my knees my fingers tugging my hair, I sit there and think. I have this insatiable need to know what she looks like. It's eating at me, how can I already be drawn to someone just by their words on a page, their voice through a shitty global phone connection.

She likes my laugh, she called me Raid, fuck I liked it when she called me Raid. When she first answered my call, she sounded quiet and unsure of herself, like she didn't think she should be talking to me but then she spoke again and I heard a confident sexy woman. Her voice was the equivalent to silk running through my fingers.

Listening to her talk, knowing she was listening to me, letting me get out what I needed to say and not shutting down on me when I approached it by scolding her dead husband... That got to me. She didn't get pissed, she seemed astonished I would blame him and not her. That's something I have to make her understand, this, everything around me, everything that happened to Garrett overseas, doesn't have anything to do with her.

She's the one that brings a man home, the one that gives a man hope at the end of the day when he has sand in his boots, dirt on his face and his muscles are achin'. She's the woman that gives a man something to take his mind off this fucking place.

I'm coming to realize now, that I didn't have anything to keep me rooted in the states, something other than my mama to come home to. And it makes me feel incredibly lonely.

Garrett had that, but will I ever have it? Meaningless sex is fun, I never really wanted more than that. I'm a ghost when I'm stateside, because this is where I belong, next to my brothers. I can't imagine having something real and passionate and then having to leave her behind to go on a mission. She wouldn't know if I would come back, when I go dark it's hard. My mama worries about me and it's sketchy, having to put her in that position in the first place. For the first time in my life, I'm left questioning my path. What always was so concrete, so set in stone is now crumbling into questions I never knew I needed answered.

Sitting up and tugging my boots on, I get up and walk outside into the dry night air. I look up at the stars and know I can't let all this go. I might have been able to before this afternoon even when I got back, I was going to end it. I was going to save her from becoming attached to me. How arrogant that sounds. Really, I'm starting to think that it's myself I was trying to protect. No strings meant I wouldn't hurt anyone if I get blown up over here.

Now I just know too much, after finding out what Garrett did, and how strong Eli is, I think I might need her more than she needs me.

This was supposed to be advice from someone who has spent time overseas, someone who can relate to her Navy SEAL husband. Now it's turning into me satisfying my need to hear her sweet voice, take her sweetness and make it my own. I know I'm being a selfish bastard, but fuck if I can stop.

Walking over to a low wall, I sit down and lean back, once again staring into the stars searching for answers.

I let my eyes travel through the darkness of space, concentrating hard, hoping that maybe if I do it long enough, her face might be there looking back down at me.

I'm still wallowing there outside, as it approaches two am, thinking about this faceless voice I can't let go when an explosion rocks my body a little too close for comfort.

Then I hear the distinct crack crack crack of automatic weapon fire. "FUCK!" I sprint into the tent, yelling at Weston to wake up when another explosion lights up the night nearly blinding us.

I yank my gear on and Weston does the same.

"What's happening Raiden?!"

"I don't know man, but we gotta get out of here." I rush out of the tent with Weston coming in hot behind me just as more gunfire sounds and we are shoved into the fray.

Chapter 9

~Elli~

"*More bad news from the front lines of Iraq tonight. A group of insurgents hit a military base on the out skirts of Baghdad early there this morning. Reports say there are three dead and several soldiers wounded. We will report more on this attack as the information comes to us. Thank you, Tom, in other news...*"

I stay frozen, facing my television. My jaw is trembling and my heart is filling with sickening dread. My ears refuse to filter in anything further.

"*Military base...Baghdad...Three dead, several wounded...*" Raiden. Oh God, Raiden.

I hear Jen in my kitchen talking to Dahlia, but I don't go to them. When I finally realize what's happened I sprint to my purse, my socks sliding on the hard wood floor. In my haste, I knock my bag to the ground, and everything spills out.

I snatch my phone up and go through my email, nothing.

I check my call log for missed phone calls. Nothing.

I dial the global cell Raiden called me on, but the call doesn't go through.

I sink to the floor surrounded by the contents of my purse, my phone sitting heavy in my hands. *Raiden.*

My sluggish mind finally processes that he might really be one of those wounded or dead and the first tear spills over my lashes and splashes down to the screen of my phone, followed by the second that hits my hand. The third and the fourth fall and then as if I'm being strangled by grief so hot and fresh, I stop being able to catch my breath.

I don't know if he's okay, I don't know if he's dead or wounded or captured. I just don't know. Once I finally shudder in a breath, despair wrapping its claws around my heart, I start sobbing. Not quietly, but loud body racking sobs.

Jen skates around the corner between the kitchen where I'm rocking myself back and forth on the floor, almost stepping on me, confusion marring her face at my sudden meltdown.

"Omg Elli, what's wrong? Honey, what happened??" I feel her hands on my back trying to soothe me and I start sobbing harder, close to the point of wailing as if my heart is dying, as if it's Garrett all over again.

Jen is doing her best to calm me down and find out what happened but I'm slipping further and further into darkness, the pain blinding me and holding me hostage.

I can't stop hearing his voice in my head, his bourbon deepness, the way he laughs, the way he said my name. How it rumbled through his lips like a reverie, a prayer.

I lean into Jen and she cradles me like a child knowing I need to find a way to stop hysterically sobbing or I'll slip into an anxiety attack.

No one can help me. I feel helpless not knowing if he's okay, this is some kind of twisted fresh hell.

Raiden.

Please call me, please email me. Please be okay... please be alive, sweetheart, I can't lose you too.

Please, I just found you.

Someone to listen to me and to understand where I'm coming from, I send my prayers up to heaven, hoping Raiden isn't already there staring down at me.

These thoughts keep playing over and over in my head. I can't do this, not after losing Garrett, I can't lose someone else to this fucking war.

I won't survive it.

I don't even let myself even think about what's happening to me right now, feeling like this over someone I've never met.

Someone I've never held.

Someone I've never kissed.

Never had the pleasure to love.

My phone rings suddenly, crashing through my sobs and I flinch in Jen's arms.

I grasp my phone and wipe my eyes to check the number, praying to God that it's him. Praying this is something good, praying that I can hear his voice again.

The anguish inside only ripping me apart further at the thought that this phone call could be the opposite, it might be too late.

I answer the number I don't recognize.

With tears in my throat, I say, "Hello?" The line crackles, but then I hear it. Like it was heaven sent I hear his voice.

"Elli, sweet girl."

A fresh wave of tears cascades down my face, my smile coming through wobbly.

"Raid, Oh God." I sniff.

He breathes into the phone what sounds like a sigh of relief.

"I needed to hear you," he says it quietly. What he doesn't realize is that I feel the same way, tears still making their tracks down my cheeks.

"I needed to hear you too, I was so terrified, they said on the news that soldiers had died and others were wounded, I didn't know what to do, Raiden." I sniff back more tears, my voice sounding watery but so relieved.

Jen is sitting there confused, her eyebrows pinched together and her head tilting to the side.

His voice comes through to me again and it's a voice I never want to take for granted.

"I can't talk long but I needed to let you know I was okay," he pauses. "I think it's more for my sanity but I couldn't not call you." It's almost like he's embarrassed.

"Raiden," I pause, "whatever your last name is," I say firmly. "You never feel embarrassed for calling me, you have no idea how much I needed you to get ahold of me. Hearing your voice right now is bringing me back to life."

Jen makes a noise next to me and her jaw pops open. I smile waiting for Raiden to respond. When he does, I swear my heart stops. His voice is so clear and deep it does something to me.

"Sweet girl, I had to get to you. I won't ever leave you in the dark if I can help it. I promise you that. I have to go now but I will email or call as soon as I can, we have some shit going down here we need to take care of."

Sweet girl, those two words light my soul on fire. I didn't realize words could do that to you.

"Okay, just be safe." I close my eyes soaking up my last minutes with him on the phone.

"And Elli?" he starts.

"Yeah?" I whisper.

"My last name is Michaels."

Then the line goes dead. *Oh, Raiden Michaels what are you doing to me?*

I take a deep breath, the first real breath since hearing the news this morning.

Jen clears her throat from beside me.

"You gonna tell me about this juicy development or what?

I giggle, my heart fuller than it has been in so so long it's almost bursting.

Two bottles of wine later and we are sufficiently drunk, at four in the afternoon. Whose idea was this again?

Jen is caught up to speed on my little friendship with Raiden and proved to be intensely supportive of it, which kind of caught me off guard.

I suppose I'm so used to being regarded a certain way, the broken damaged way, that I find it odd when people don't treat me like that.

Raiden doesn't and Jen never has, which I needed to remember.

When you're shattered into a million little pieces it doesn't matter if the love and support has been there along. At least not until you are picked up enough to notice who is standing there in solidarity beside you.

In my drunk state, listening to Jen humming along to Ellie Goulding I bob my head, for the first time in what feels like an eon letting myself be free from the burden of Garrett's death. Something that is always with me is suddenly a lot easier to deal with.

I'm getting up to get another bottle opened when Ellie just speaks to me singing about having someone on her mind.

I spin around nearly falling down, shouting "OMG Jen, this is me right now. Like I don't even get it, he's on my mind all the time! It doesn't make sense!"

I'm badly slurring my words but who cares?

I'm happy and drunk and Ellie Goulding is telling me exactly what is going on in my head right now.

We start scream-singing the lyrics until we end up in a pile on the couch, our sides aching from laughing so hard. Jen props herself up, all pink cheeked and wide eyed, looking like she is going to spill out a revelation.

"Oh no, what are you think...thinking you sneaky lady." I level her gaze as best I can but there are two of her where there should be one.

"Okay, so like Raiden doesn't know what you look like...right?"

I narrow my eyes at her, or her general direction anyway.

"Uh, yeah and I don't know what he looks like either." Still narrowing my eyes, trying to follow her train of thought. She holds up her hands almost falling over in the process.

"Hear me out...let's take a selfie."

My eyes get big and my face splits into a huge grin, how had I not thought of this sooner! Best drunk plan ever.

I grab my phone and click the camera app, aiming it at us I take four pictures. The first two were blurry, of course, due to the drunk.

The last two were okay but looking between them I find the one I really like. My hair looks good, my face is bright, a little pink but I am smiling so hard I almost can't believe it.

I haven't seen myself look this...*alive* since before Garrett died. I don't know who this Elli is but I think I love her.

I attach the photo to an email titled "Ellie Goulding" and all I say is, "Cause I got you on my mind" and click send.

Descending into wine drunk madness we delight in our perfect drunk selfie and relax into a pile on the couch.

Chapter 10

~Raiden~

Base is still a mess. I've been working non-stop with the guys trying to get it put back together but we were hit really hard.

The news reported that "Three were dead and several wounded." The several wounded part was correct, there were, however, none that died.

They showed pictures of "fallen soldiers" when in reality they were fucking insurgents dressed in uniform.

Anyone could see that those were not our men, but America needs its daily dose of carnage and gore.

I was beyond pissed when I found that shit out because I know now that Elli saw it and it worried her. I was okay, but of course she hadn't known that and she...she cried for me. She didn't tell me so, but I could hear it in her broken voice that she had been crying. This beauty, crying over a poor sap stuck in the desert. I have to be the luckiest guy alive.

I run my hand up and down the back of my neck. I'm covered head to toe in crusted dirt and sand. I need a shower badly, but I need to check on Elli more. It's been two days since I was able to get in touch with her and I swear hearing her voice was like heaven calling me home. I thought I had truly died and gone there just hearing her answer, her concern for me doing something to my stomach, making it do some kind of backflip. Hearing something like that come from that sexy silky voice, I got rock hard. Zero to one hundred in about two nanoseconds.

This woman does shit to me I can't even control it.

What's more is I don't want to.

I sneak into the damaged but functional comm tent and boot up the computer, anxiously bouncing my leg up and down, wanting to contact my girl.

Fuck, *mine*?

I know she isn't yet but I'm gonna make her mine, how can I not with how I feel?

Not after all this, it has only been a couple weeks but it feels like I've known her a lot longer.

I know such intimate damaged details about her. It just feels like more. So much more.

Opening my email, I sigh a happy full breath seeing I have one from her. The title gives me pause, not quite understanding it. But shit, I'm too excited to dick around about opening it so I click open.

It asks me if I want to download attachment.

Attachment?

Oh, I hope it's her, I want to see what I'm sure is the most beautiful angel.

Please, please, please.

Feeling like these twenty seconds are taking twenty years I clench and unclench my fists on my thighs.

It opens and I lose all sense of my surroundings.

I can't hear anything, I can't feel anything and I can't see anything but her.

My body fills with a white hot fire starting in my toes, brushing past my rock hard cock and settling deep in my chest like it's found a home and wants to burn there forever.

I knew she was gonna be a beautiful angel but she is... absolutely beyond words.

She is without a doubt the most fucking perfect, literal breathtaking woman I have ever seen.

She has long white blonde hair, the bluest eyes and the most adorable and sexy pink cheeks. Her teeth so white and straight, her lips just slightly pouty, enough to make my cock pulse in my pants thinking sinful thoughts about what they would feel like wrapped around me.

It's like white noise in my ears and I can't focus on anything but how unbelievably gorgeous she is.

Pausing, realizing I didn't read what she wrote along with the picture, I scan through the only sentence she wrote, "'Cause I got you on my mind."

I get fist punched right in my chest, knowing this heaven sent woman is thinking about me. All my previous thoughts come thundering back, practically knocking me over.

My sweet girl.

Mine.

I hit print on the picture, and tap a reply before I have to go return to the fresh hell that is our base of operations, after witnessing what heaven looks like firsthand.

To: norwegianbeauty@gmail.com
From: usmcraider1@gmail.com
Subject: Re: Ellie Goulding

Sweet girl,

You're always on my mind. And know that now I'll be able to carry you around with me wherever I go.

-Raid

I hit send, wearing a smile so big it's busting my cheeks.

I walk out of the tent, my body feeling lighter than air, my dick still rock hard. Just a simple picture has me so hard I could quite literally pound nails.

Just one look at this woman and I feel like my heart's been hijacked.

This feeling is unlike anything I have ever felt, this possessive need to make her mine and never let anyone steal her light again.

Quicksand

I tuck Elli into my pocket and count the hours until I'll be able to push everything else aside and just stare at her.

Chapter 11

~Elli~

Something just beeped.
I open my eyes just a sliver, the light assaulting my poor retinas immediately.

I slam them closed and hear what I can only guess as my phone beep again. I forget for two seconds I'm suffering from the worst wine hangover known to man and try to sit bolt upright hoping that it's an email from Raiden.

I instantly regret the rapid movement and groan, my hands coming up to cover my face. I keep my eyes closed and feel around for my phone as if I didn't have the use of my eyes at all. My fingers bump into it wedged between the couch cushion and the face of my best friend.

I giggle, Jen isn't waking up anytime soon if the snoring is any indication. I settle back down on the couch next to my bestie and open my eyes only enough to see the screen, but not all the way so I have to deal with the screaming pain that is my wine hungover-ed head.

I see an email notification so I click it, my excitement overriding how shitty I feel.

My eyes scan through it over and over. The words ricocheting around in my head, making me feel all the feels.

"Sweet girl...I'll be able to carry you around with me."

I feel that feeling that had settled low in my belly spread its wings and fly straight into my heart, my stomach fluttering with all the good feelings I have so desperately and recklessly missed. Raiden put them there...

I close my eyes and thoughts of Garrett suddenly assault me.

Lately, all I can do is think about Raid, but I still have another man in my life.

My husband.

Tears sting the back of my eyes, and I'm glad Jen's still sleeping because I need to process this alone.

How do you let in someone new when you've been utterly consumed by someone for so long?

Am I allowed to let myself feel like this?

I still wear the guilt from Garrett's death as some sort of widow shroud, will it ever lift?

I take in a shaky breath, the tears slipping out and coating my eyelashes.

Garrett, honey I miss you so much. The words I so desperately want to say out loud only whisper through my mind.

I feel my heart aching at the loss of my husband once more, the crushing pain I avoided by focusing on Raiden and how he makes me feel once again holds me prisoner.

I get up slowly and softly pad up the stairs to my bedroom, closing the door behind me.

I curl up in the middle of the big bed and let my eyes close, wanting to talk this out to him in silence, something I should have done long before this.

Why did you leave me?

I let the tears come hard and fast, coming like the first downpour of a summer storm. *Garrett, I don't know how to start over.*

How do I navigate this life without you?

Why did you go, I could've helped you, baby, I would've listened to you.

The tears start pooling around my face in the comforter, and I shakily exhale my sorrow. *You were my brave, protective guy.*

You kept me safe and warm and loved and then you left me, cold and alone. You left me mentally even before you were physically gone and that hurt. You hurt me. Garrett, why did you do this to me? Why did you leave me by myself, honey... Why can't I have you back, what could I have done. "What could I have done..." I sob out.

I'm so mad at you... because I have been so lost without you. Garrett, you were my anchor keeping me from floating away and then you disappeared and

I floated. I floated for two years before I reached the shore until I reached the sand. Now I can't even let myself be happy experiencing these feelings because I am still so... fucking mad at you.

My lips tremble as I wage a silent war between myself and my dead husband's memory, my tears coming hard and fast while the dam of feelings I try to keep in finally bursts.

I need someone to save me, Garrett. Show me I deserve to be saved, please baby.

A tremor rocks through my body, which I send my pleading prayer to him up in heaven, needing with all of my shattered soul to be able to know it's okay.

I need to know that I deserve this. That I'm not a horrible person for wanting to let go and be happy again.

I lie there in a ball, holding myself together because I know if I let go I would break apart again and never be put back together. I hold myself because no one else is here to do it for me. I clutch my sides until my fingers ache. I breathe a little deeper, my tears coming slower now. I need to sleep, I'm so exhausted. If I sleep I don't have to stay in this reality. I don't have to feel this pain anymore. Maybe if I give in and let sleep take me, I can be happy again. I can only hope.

I stay like that until I drift off to sleep, and then I dream.

I dream it's my wedding day again.

I'm getting ready to meet my dad and have him walk me down the aisle, taking one last look in the mirror, I conclude that I'm stunning.

My long curly blonde hair done to perfection, my makeup light and even more perfect. But the smile, the smile is what really catches my attention. I am so inexplicably happy that it shines through my every pore.

I turn and walk to my dad, taking his arm and moving forward. I look down as I make it to the very beginning of the aisle, and breathe deep. Happiness radiating from me like a thousand tiny stars shining brightly.

I keep my eyes trained down as dad walks me down the aisle until it's finally time to look up. We come to a gentle halt and I look up, so ready to meet the eyes of my soon to be husband.

Except when I try to meet his eyes I can't see them.

They aren't my Garrett's familiar gorgeous green orbs that are watching me take my place across from him, my hands in his. I can't even make out his features, but I'm not upset, I am still just as radiantly happy, if not more.

The minister says his piece as we stand there hand in hand, our families crying tears of joy and wonderment. I feel a warm light surround me as I say "I do" and a feeling of absolute calm washes over me. I beam at my almost husband, my heart swelling, full to bursting.

I can almost feel myself smiling in my sleep, knowing I'm waking up but wanting to live in this unbridled bliss a moment longer.

The last thing I remember before I surface is hearing Raiden's voice saying, "I do, sweet girl, I do."

I open my eyes, still lying in the middle of my bed but feeling that warm blanket of calm surrounding me.

A few tears seep out of the sides of my eyes, but this time the tears aren't of pain and anguish. They're tears of acceptance and gratitude.

Gratitude to my beloved husband because even in death he gave me what I needed to take the first steps in letting go and moving on.

Chapter 12

~Elli~

I laid in the center of my huge bed for what seemed like centuries, my soul somewhere between beginning to heal and still shrouded in despair.

I know having a dream as monumental as that should mean everything to me, but it's hard because it does and it doesn't.

Garrett was and is still so much my whole life, but that dream felt like I should be moving forward, not stay glued to the spot in the past.

Am I too damaged?

I don't even know if Raiden feels that way for me, I know that we flirt here and there but he is so far away, he could just be lonely.

I can't honestly believe someone would want me after all of this, all of this misery I've come to live in, and after everything I've told him, what if he wants to turn and run the other way. There's also the fact he's so far away from me and if I'm being honest with myself the fact he's probably Special Ops scares the hell out of me.

He hasn't outright said it but he isn't super forthcoming with what he is actually doing over there and it reminds me of Garrett. That means he goes dark for months too, goes into the most dangerous situations, could end up so torn up that he doesn't want to live anymore....

I roll onto my back and stare up at the ceiling, letting out a big breath.

Where do I even start?

This hurt I've lived in every day for two long years has become my home. Telling Raiden about Garrett was hard but it felt good to get it off my chest.

It's nearly comical how I can be so totally consumed by something so horrible and damaging that it is both all I can talk about and everything I don't want to talk about.

I hear my door crack open just a sliver and turn my head to see a pair of hazel, bloodshot eyes staring at me curiously.

"Hey baby girl, you doing okay in here?"

Jen pushes the door open a little more so I can see how haggard and silly she looks, which causes a small smile to ghost my lips.

"Come here, bestie."

She comes in and lies next to me, taking my hand in hers and squeezing.

"Hey E?"

I look at her and see nothing but solid tangible love and determination shining back at me.

"What's up, honey?"

She looks at me hard and says quietly, "I know it's gonna be hard, and I know you are not anywhere near where you need to be but you have to do this for yourself."

She pauses to make sure it's sinking in, and it is. It really is.

"You have been on the last page of your book for a long time sweetie, it's time to write the final sentence and move on to the sequel."

A tear escapes my eye and slides down my cheek, her own eyes shining with unshed tears as well.

"Last night I felt my best friend coming back to me, you were so light and free, I just know you have to try babe, you have to do this on your own terms but you HAVE to do this." She squeezes my hand one last time and just before she gets up and backs out my door says, "Going to get us hungover-ed bitches some Starbucks," then disappears out into the hall.

I roll back over to gaze up at the dimmed glow in the dark stars on my ceiling and wish with everything inside me that I could just let all of this go. That I knew how to fight anymore. As I'm contemplating how to get my ass into gear with becoming a whole person again, a star suddenly unsticks and lands in one of my upturned palms.

I sit up and hold it like it's some sort of sign, knowing this has to be some sort of cosmic push.

I set it on my nightstand and swing my gaze to the closet.

I cautiously walk over to it like it's harboring some kind of ghoulish monster.

Opening the French doors that conceal so much of my life behind them, I take a deep inhale and am instantly surrounded by him.

I walk in, flipping on the light and gather my strength to stare at Garrett's clothes. I run my hands over his Naval uniforms, both formal and combat. He always looked so perfectly rugged and put together all at once when he was in uniform.

Moving on to his T-shirts and jeans, I think about all the times we would just do random things to make our home more *us*, getting into paint fights and hanging pictures lopsided because I was too impatient to use a level.

I move closer to his clothes, faintly smelling his sexy smell, wishing desperately there was a hard body under the clothes that I could touch, hold on to forever. I grab a decent amount of fabric and hug it close to me, letting my eyes drift close and in a rare moment, let myself miss him like I want to. I miss him every day of my life but I don't get to express it truly, let myself feel the enormity of missing someone who isn't living anymore, just like last night. I'm washed away in a riptide of memories, both good and bad. The good are glorious, days where we couldn't keep our hands off each other, our wedding day, the day we first met and how hard he pursued me until I fell in love with him. How much I missed him and despised the days he had to leave for deployment, how proud and overjoyed I was when he came home. The bad seeps in between the good, poisoning the happiness that coursed through me for only a moment. The fights, the distance, how desperate I began to feel every day. The thoughts of the love of my life were slipping away from me.

I clutch Garrett's clothes tighter, my fists closing hard around sleeves causing my knuckles to ache.

Don't think about it Elli, don't let yourself go there.

I do anyway, like a car wreck I'm unable not to think about it.

Garrett's blood.

My gun.

The man of my dreams lying there so lifeless.

I let my tears fall, soaking through one of his shirts, mixing parts of us together.

Then I get upset, I revert back to the easiest form of emotion I can find, anger.

I stand back and feel nothing but heartbreak and anguish.

How dare he leave me here alone!

How dare he do this to me!

I only see white-hot rage, I start wrenching clothing from the hangers, slinging them to the floor. I let out a frustrated scream-growl and let out all my angst on his clothes. I stand back once I'm done and take in the wreckage around me.

I did this.

I ripped apart his memory...

What have I done?

Collapsing down on the pile of Garrett's clothing, I let myself fall to pieces once more.

How often can I do this before someone locks me up? I know this isn't normal or healthy. I'm fighting a goddamn ghost that won't stop haunting me. The worst part is...I don't want him to.

I snuggle into the mangled pieces of my husband and let myself drift, hoping this time when I do that I won't see the end of him, but hoping against all hope that I could understand what was happening to my Garrett even when I know it's impossible.

My breathing halts for a second, remembering that the whole reason why I messaged Raiden was to understand. What he's given me isn't gruesome sorted details of combat but he's given me something to look forward to. Something to make my smile light up.

I look around the wreckage and realize this wasn't a breakdown, this was a breakthrough.

Chapter 13

~Raiden~

I'd only been sleeping for about an hour when I hear Weston mumbling somewhere to my left. My ears perk up only slightly, making sure nothing's wrong. A habit I've become accustomed to, being alert no matter if you're sleeping, awake, doesn't matter. You have to be on your A game at every moment over here, or you end up dead. Period.

The only problem is it sounds like West is having a bad dream. He normally doesn't talk or mumble in his sleep but I can hear him loud and clear and it sounds like he's warring with something in his dreams.

I sit up slowly, rubbing my exhausted eyes and turn his way. He's tossing around on his cot, and even from my side of the tent, I can see he's covered in a thick sheen of sweat.

I slip my feet into my boots and pad over to him, reaching out a tentative hand to his shoulder.

He comes up swinging when I make contact, but thankfully I was planning on something like this so I jumped back before he hit me.

His eyes shoot open and he turns every which way looking bewildered.

He lets out a frustrated growl, "Raiden what the fuck?!"

I can't help but to scowl at him, but quickly soothe my expression knowing he was just having a nightmare.

"You were talking in your sleep man, you good?"

I stare hard at him, and then soften again showing my genuine concern.

"Yeah, yeah man, I'm good."

He scrubs his hands down his face and then lays back and rolls over, turning away from me.

I go back to my own cot and sit down, my elbows on my knees, my fists propping my head up under my chin.

I wonder what he was dreaming about, I can only guess, but I'm thinking he's reliving something. We've been fortunate enough in the tours we've had together that we haven't lost many of the brothers fighting along with us but that doesn't mean we haven't seen some heavy shit. I haven't had many nightmares where I relive something we've gone through but when I do… it fucking blows. You feel helpless seeing such carnage and terror, not being able to put a stop to it, save a civilian… anything.

That's honestly the worst part about the nightmares, that you can't do anything to stop it. I can't imagine if something happened in the field and you had that weighing on your conscience, so when you dreamt, you had nightmares of that. I don't know what it's like to lose a brother in the same battle I'm in and I hope against hope I'll never experience it. Like I said, we've been lucky. As concerned as I am for my best friend I can't help that my thoughts turn to Elli. I slide my boots back off and lay back down on my cot, my arms going to rest behind my head, my eyes scanning the ceiling of our tent.

I wonder if something like that happened to Garrett in the field.

Maybe he lost one of his buddies and it weighed too heavy on his mind, couldn't escape it. I still can't figure out how he could leave that sweet woman behind, leave this world in such a way and have her find him.

I close my eyes, a grimace on my face. I wish she wouldn't have gone through that, I know it had fucked her up in the head. Not in a way that she can't recover but I can just imagine she's struggling with how I've been to her. Calling her sweet girl, flirting.

She said it's been two years since he died and she's still wearing her widow shroud.

Is it bad I want to rescue her?

Take her away from all the pain she forces herself to live in every day?

I sigh, heavy and burdened. Realizing I won't be getting back to sleep anytime soon, I sit up again and don my boots, heading over to the comm tent.

All I want to do is talk to her, reach out to her, get some stuff off my own chest.

I just hope she'll listen to what I'm saying, and more importantly that I won't scare her off.

Quicksand

To: norwegianbeauty@gmail.com
From: usmcraider1@gmail.com
Subject: Can't Sleep

Hey sweet girl,

My buddy Weston woke me up after barely getting any sleep in the first place. He's having nightmares and I have to be honest... it's worrying me.

I asked him if he's good and he said he was, so I won't press it but it still weighs on me. How are you?

Tell me about you Elli.

I want to know you.

I want you to take my mind away from this place, take me back to California.

I'll tell you more about me too, so it's fair.

My middle name is Edward. Raiden Edward Michaels.

I am twenty-eight years old and basically live with my mama, don't laugh I have my own place but don't stay at it often.

My favorite color is blue and even though I don't always get to, I like to read. Something interesting about that is I like to read about history. You can probably guess I like reading about wars in the past, but it's just tactics I study. What they could have done, what they did and didn't do.

I know I'm rambling through this email but I just needed to send you something.

I said before, I'm glad you emailed me the first time and I am, because Elli, I think I needed someone to talk to as well.

Will you do me a favor?

Listen to "The Light" by Disturbed. I think you'll like it. Really listen to the words.

Yours, Raid.

I click send, not really sure if that even made sense.

There's something about this girl, this incredible woman.

I just feel the constant aching need to reach out to her.

Throwing in the song suggestion at the end was impromptu but I think she'll get something out of it, maybe understand what I already know about her and what she needs to know about herself.

Chapter 14

~Elli~

"*Do me a favor? Listen to 'The Light' by Disturbed...*"

I smirk, interested as to why Raiden is having me listen to a band notorious for their hard beats and deep vocals.

I pop a new tab open in Chrome and YouTube it. The cover looks eerily optimistic for being close to heavy metal.

The beginning has me already feeling uplifted, when the guitar starts, I know I just found my new anthem. This song is amazing. I feel like he's singing about my life, my fears keeping me blinded.

Raiden gets me.

I bob my head along, following the lyrics on the screen, turning up the volume on my MacBook.

I tap out an email to Raiden, letting the words filter through my ears and right down to pool in my soul, giving me another piece of strength to add to my rapidly growing collection.

To: usmcraider1@gmail.com
From: norwegianbeauty@gmail.com
Subject: Disturbed

Raiden,

Thank you for this, somehow you knew exactly what I needed.

You gonna be my light, Raid?

-E

I smile, pleased with myself and feeling on a total high. It is the perfect mix of being the inspiration and motivation I need to keep moving forward while kicking absolute ass with the guitar and bass.

I buy it in iTunes, and put it on repeat, memorizing the words.

Raiden is my light. Or rather he's showing me the light I have been missing all this time.

I lean my head back against my pillows and let the vocals wash over me, familiarizing myself with the words and feeling really light.

When it goes on repeat for the third time I look down at my screen and see an email from a certain Marine sitting there waiting for me to open it.

To: norwegianbeauty@gmail.com
From: usmcraider1@gmail.com
Subject: Light

Elli,

I was hoping you would like it, every time I hear it I think of you.

You're your own light, sweet girl.

-Raid

This man.
This man knows exactly what to say to me.

Now I have a song that I can listen to whenever I want to feel empowered. Something to stave off feeling like a basket case, and one that will remind me of a certain Marine serving overseas.

I certainly want to be my own light, and in some ways, I know that I'm the only one that can pull me out of this funk, but sometimes I wonder...how can I?

How can I pick up and leave Garrett in the past?

I don't think I will ever be able to move past his monumental impact on my life, he was my everything.

I want to be strong, and sometimes I think I'm doing pretty okay.

But then there are other times that I feel that my broken parts are showing and everyone is staring at them.

I wonder if Raiden likes the strong version I try and project over email, or if he would be okay with the scarred real me.

It's easy to pretend I'm normal over the computer, maybe forget for a little while that I am merely walking around as half a person. That sometimes the grief over not having Garrett with me is all consuming and I get moody and don't smile, don't eat, don't breathe.

Maybe I should ask him, cut the bullshit. Show him the Elli that not everyone sees, the Elli that is still such a shell of a person that maybe there isn't anything left at all.

He is so sweet to me, he deserves at least to know the me that I truly am.

To: usmcraider1@gmail.com
From: norwegianbeauty@gmail.com
Subject: RE: Light

Raiden,

To answer your earlier questions, I'm doing better.
My middle name is Avery. Elli Avery Hendricks. Which is Garrett's last name, my maiden name is Bjorgo.
I am twenty-six years old and I was actually born in Norway, Stavanger to be exact. My family came to California when I was five so I remember being there, and it was beautiful, there's nothing like it.

But I guess that's the same with California, it is my second favorite place in the whole world.

Raiden... I know I keep going back and forth between happy and playful, and sad and depressing. But I can be honest with you, right? I have to be.

You make me smile, you should know that. I smile big because of you. But then I feel guilty for smiling because of you and not being torn apart at that moment by the death of my husband.

In some ways, I want to move on so badly, and then in other ways, I feel that there is no way to do it.

I know I must sound so totally fucked up, and I am, I can admit that. But I can tell just talking to you brings out the happy, it is hard to deal with after living as an empty shell for so long, but you bring it out.

That is partially why I struggle so much with it, it's hard for me to let myself smile, let myself laugh and be happy that someone so far away is taking time out of their day to email me, to call me, to console me... constantly.

I don't really know what will happen if we keep talking like this, but I think I want to find out. I just ask...be patient with me...please.

Because I think in my darkness, I'm finally seeing some light.

-Elli

Now that it's all out there in the open, I want to take it back.

I typed it all out so quickly and hit send just as fast.

I knew if I let myself review any of it I wouldn't get it out.

This had to happen, it had to be said.

I let him know how much he makes me smile and that scares me.

What scares me more is the thought of him not wanting to talk to me anymore because of the head case I am.

Who would want to take on that kind of baggage…?

God, but I want him to.

There's something about him that speaks to the secret parts of me that are still able to desire.

After all, I am still a woman, still someone who still secretly yearns to be treated like she matters again. Regarded as someone worth loving and taking a risk on.

I can't take being broken like this all the time.

I want to be worth it, I want to be something more than a widow.

I stand up and walk over to my mirror, a full-length reflection of Eli looking back at me with ice blue eyes.

I have to be stronger than this. I have my best friend here whenever I need her, and I have someone who calls me sweet girl, oceans away…but he's there. He comforts me and makes me smile.

I have to be stronger than this.

Steeling my resolve, I swing my gaze to my closet once more.

Taking a fortifying step forward, I open the doors and turn on the light. Seeing the destruction left over from my most recent breakdown, I know what needs to be done. It's merely a baby step, but it's a step that needs to be made. It's been two years, this is just one piece that I think I can let go of, even if I can't let him go completely I can take back a sliver of control in my life.

I sink to my knees and start folding Garrett's clothes, bringing some of them up to smell one last time, all the while feeling an innate sense of calm crashing over me, like I can really do this.

Jen pops her head in the door and gasps so loudly I'm surprised she didn't choke.

"Whatcha doing, girlfriend? You okay?"

She's cautious, like I'm some sort of feral animal who could snap at any second, which only really does one thing for me. Make my decision that much more concrete.

I need to change, I need to just put my big girl panties on and saddle up, this is my life and I need to be in control, not just skating by pretending to live.

I throw her a smile, a blinding megawatt smile and say, "Yeah babe, can you get me some bags? We need to make a run to the VA."

I can tell she's still in shock because she just side eyes me and walks out backward, narrowing her gaze until I can't see her anymore.

Sigh.

This is right.

I needed to start coming back to myself many moons ago but I guess better late than never, yeah?

I rock back on my heels and go to my sound bar, Bluetooth connecting my phone and start blasting a certain song I can't get out of my head, turning up the volume loud enough to drown out everything else.

Jen comes back in to help and within an hour, we have all of Garrett's clothes (minus his Uniforms because I just can't get rid of those) loaded up in my Mustang and we are speeding toward the VA.

Originally, I didn't think of going to the VA, I thought maybe just Goodwill or the Salvation Army would suffice, but the more I thought about it, the more the VA called to me. My dad was a Navy SEAL, my granddad a P.T Boat Commander in WWII, and even my grandmother served as a nurse in Pearl Harbor. I have such a strong and proud history of vets in my family that it only makes sense to give back to people that don't always get treated right. Can you imagine fighting a war for your country and coming back to no job, no benefits, not one single ounce of help when you have already given up so much? It breaks my damn heart. My family had been somewhat lucky that they never had to deal with being treated anything less than they deserved, aside from Garrett.

Veteran's affairs are so overlooked that it makes me sick, hopefully providing gently used clothing to people that can use them will make their day a little brighter.

I pull into the parking lot at the VA and look over at Jen, twisting in my seat and she's there, looking right back at me.

"I think I need to start being more involved, Jen."

She squints. "More involved in....?"

I nod once. "In Veteran's Affairs, in my life and in moving forward." I nod once more and cross my arms over my chest, determination set.

Chapter 15

~Raiden~

I'm sitting there staring at the screen of a computer, in Iraq, a whole world away from this woman and she is affecting me in such a way I'm surprised she isn't right here with me.

It's like she knows exactly what to say to fist punch me right in the heart, steal all my breath and make me ache in a way that feels nothing short of pure agony.

She thinks she's fucked up... She still blames herself. She just can't see, can she?

She can't see that's why she feels guilty for talking to me, I mean, fucking hell she feels guilty for smiling?

I know I can't fix her, but I don't want to.

I want her to find her way into the light and then let it wash through her, take away all her hurt.

She doesn't deserve to live in a perpetual hell that was created by someone when they left this world.

I shake my head, knowing I need to get going back to my tent and at least get some sort of sleep before I have to go out and be a soldier.

To: norwegianbeauty@gmail.com
From: usmcraider1@gmail.com
Subject: Here

Elli girl,

I'm here.

-Raid

I hit send and shut down the computer, dragging my feet out of the comm tent.

I look up at those stars again, letting myself wish that this whole situation was different. Why couldn't I be wanting a woman who wasn't so scared to let herself want again, let herself live again.

Why do I even feel like this for her? I reach down into my pocket and pull out her picture, her smile warming my heart, how beautiful she is. I can't be her hero because she needs to be a hero for herself, but I can do my best to protect her from any more pain and anguish...

Assuming I even get to see her when I come off tour.

This could all just be a fantasy between a sweet broken woman and a soldier overseas. I take in her soft features, her blonde hair, her icy blue eyes so like mine but so much more feminine.

Where I'm all dark, she's all light. Her nose small, her lips just a little pouty and entirely kissable. A set of lips I'd love nothing more than to take in between my teeth and run my tongue over...

Jesus, what am I even thinking?

Staring down at the situation rising in my pants, becoming more painful by the minute, I realize two things. I am very attracted to Eli, and I am a very long way away from her. I walk back to my tent and drop onto my cot, exhausted, horny and wishing that California was a fuck of a lot closer.

"Good shootin' out there, Michaels! You saved our asses today, man!" Gage shouts my way, as I'm shuffling my aching feet back toward mine and Weston's tent.

"I got you, brother!" I yell back, dipping my sand and sweat soaked head into what we call home over here.

I shrug off my gear and strip down, a shower the only thing on my mind.

I get done, finally washing off the day, glad as shit we all made it back to base in one piece, another day down and no one died, it's a good day.

I head into the comm tent, another ritual I've started, checking my email every chance I get, which I'll admit, is exhausting.

My drive to talk to Elli every chance I get is entirely insatiable, a craving I suddenly formed and can't seem to kick, like I even want to.

I have three emails waiting for me from Elli, which both makes me unbelievably happy and unsettles me at the same time, I hope everything's good with her.

To: usmcraider1@gmail.com
From: norwegianbeauty@gmail.com
Subject: VA

Hi,

I want to apologize for my last email, Raid...I kind of had to get that all out there at once and I hope that it didn't scare you...

I feel more alive talking to you than I have in two years, and I just... I don't know I just want to be completely transparent with you.

SO, after I sent that last email I had a little epiphany and I neatly folded all of Garrett's clothes and took them to the VA, where I am pleased to tell you I now work.

I also forgot to mention I'm a paramedic, well I was before all of...that went down.

Anyway, they're letting me do intake and vitals on their patients who come through there, vets coming in for check-ups and such, which honestly makes me really happy. I needed to be doing something other than wallowing.

Stay safe,

-Eli

I lean back, a huge smile on my face, almost taking up the whole of it.

Go Eli!

A complete one-eighty from her last email, I'm pleased she's doing this for herself and she seems so happy, bonus.

It's incredibly sexy she's a paramedic, I thought she was hot before, but now it's like a whole different level of smoking.

Just imagining her in her little uniform, racing around, high on adrenaline...my cock pulses, desperately needing attention.

Yeah, I know buddy.

I click to open her second email, one that by the looks of it, she only sent about twenty minutes ago.

To: usmcraider1@gmail.com
From: norwegianbeauty@gmail.com
Subject: Hyper

Raiden,

I just had the BEST DAY and I couldn't wait to message you about it. You were the first person I wanted to tell.

I met five people today who truly touched me, it made my whole week just being able to talk with them and hear their stories.

I think everyone needs this kind of support, people willing to listen to them and really hear them.

I hope you're doing okay over there, I miss being able to IM you, you must be out in the field a lot, you better be staying safe. *Picture a grumpy face*

I'm taking this new Elli day-by-day, baby steps and all. But it feels so fabulous to actually be getting back to me, and doing what I love.

I even told the VA that I'll work for minimum wage, Garrett's pension keeps me comfortable anyway and I like helping soldiers and their families, it's more than enough of a reward for me.

-Elli

God, she's so cute.

I can practically feel how excited she is just by how she's wording her email, wishing I could hear her sweet sexy voice telling me about her day instead of reading it.

I open the last one only sent five minutes ago, my pulse ratcheting up as I see the subject line. *Skype?*

To: usmcraider1@gmail.com
From: norwegianbeauty@gmail.com
Subject: Skype?

Raid,

I actually have no clue what you look like... Maybe you could Skype me sometime?

-E

It takes me seconds to spring into action, hoping she hasn't gone offline already.

The thought of actually seeing her live and being able to talk to her while seeing her face absolutely thrills me.

I hastily login, my hands flying across the keyboard like they're on fire.

It makes a noise when I add her by name, thanking God we told each other our full names.

I click to connect to her, seeing she's online, hopefully waiting for me, with a touch of nervousness sliding into my throat.

The seconds seemingly span into an eternity and then...then there she is.

Elli.

My sweet beautiful girl.

A huge grin splits my face and a feeling similar to soaring takes root in my heart.

She smiles at me, giving a little wave and gracing me with her voice.

"Hi Raiden."

I'm mesmerized by her, her hair in a messy bun on the top of her head, purple reading glasses on, not a hint of makeup, *flawless.*

She's wearing a big T-shirt and shorts, her tan legs folded into a pretzel in front of her, sitting on her bed. She's comfortable and sexy all in one tight little blonde package.

She takes her lip in between her teeth as she assesses me back, reminding me for the first time that until now she didn't know what I looked like.

I straighten up so she can see as much of me as possible in the web cam, even trying to impress her a little by bringing my arms up to rest on the back of my neck, flexing my biceps. My voice is husky and deep when I finally speak, knowing that above all else what I say is the truth.

"Elli, you're so fucking beautiful."

Chapter 16

~Elli~

"*Elli, you're so fucking beautiful.*"

If someone asked me ten minutes ago what my favorite sound was, I would've said something stupid like the ocean.

But now, I know without one shred of doubt my favorite sound is my name coming from Raiden Michaels' lips.

The way he says it with a hint of disbelief makes me feel unbelievable.

I'm blushing and I'm speechless, my thoughts racing a million miles an hour.

Raiden Edward Michaels is a fucking god.

I thought I was going to faint when I clicked accept on the Skype call just from sheer anticipation, nervousness, and curiosity.

Then I was sure I was going to pass out when he filled up my computer screen.

His eyes are so like mine, but deeper, more masculine, like the Atlantic Ocean, so blue and so endless.

His dark eyelashes are on the longer side, adding to the melt factor.

His hair is closely cut and dark, but long enough to where I could run my fingers through it if I wanted to, and God, I so want to.

His jaw is strong and dusted in a light stubble, which completely hikes up the melt factor, leaving me in a big pile of female hormones.

Just as I'm admiring how handsome he is, he does something so simple, that cranks up his perfection tenfold.

He brings his hands up to rest behind his neck, his big biceps flexing and effectively making my mouth water. It's then that I get to study some of the many tattoos he has running up and down his skin.

I make a mental note to ask him about them later.

I can't make them out perfectly, but they're intricate and there is nothing more I would like to do than trace each and every one with my tongue. At this, I blush hard, surprised at my train of thought.

I have to speak. I have to do more than just stare at him like a horny teenager, as much as I could just stare at him for eternity.

Sigh.

Of course, I go for the most awkward question I could think of.

"Raid… why are you so sweet to me?"

I cringe, knowing how weird that sounded but hey! I am genuinely interested in this.

He smirks and brings his arms down, much to my dismay, moving to lean in closer to the web cam so I have an up close and personal view of his handsome face, making me feel hot all over.

"Because I can't help myself."

He looks down at his hands for a beat then looks back up, searing me with his gaze.

Ugh, the smolder.

"You make it easier being over here."

A whoosh of air leaves my lungs and just like that, I'm speechless again.

It's right then that I have another epiphany.

I can be myself with him, I can flirt, I can show him I care, this is allowed, I am a single woman for crying out loud!

"Well, you know what? You make it really hard being over here."

I adjust my purple reading glasses on my face and smirk, trying and failing, unable to keep a stern look.

He starts laughing, something that is already becoming one of my favorite sounds.

"So Elli, now that you know what I look like, what do you think?"

He winks, and if my panties weren't already on fire, that would have done it.

Spontaneous combustion much?

"Well..." I look down, trying to be playful, "I guess you're like okay or something..."

I hide my mouth behind my hands so he doesn't see the uncontrollable smile threatening to give me away.

He narrows his eyes at me and cocks an eyebrow.

"Okay or something?"

I can't help it, I bust up laughing, falling over onto my side on my bed.

Meanwhile, Raiden just stares at me, a look of utter amusement crossing his face.

"Raid, come on, you're to fucking die for."

My eyes get big at my confession, way surprised with how frank I was with him, which then causes me to blush even harder, pretty embarrassed.

With my face hidden in my hands, I hear chuckling and when I look up, I see him doubled over laughing.

"Well, pretty girl, I am so glad you think so."

Cue another panty melting smile.

"Now, how about you tell me about your day."

He asks me all the right questions over the next twenty minutes and in that time I learned he actually tolerates tofu, likes to grill with his shirt off (no complaints if that ever happens when I'm around), and his favorite car is a '69 Chevy Camaro. Which makes me laugh because even though my Mustang is the newest model, we are both clearly into muscle cars.

I got to stare at him while he spoke, so full of life, using hand gestures and smiling, his deep voice bounding from the screen.

I told him about how much I love being a paramedic, but how different it is after not working very often over the last two years. Garrett's pension from the military kept me afloat when I was too unstable to work and it almost allowed me to wallow longer, knowing I wouldn't lose my house.

But working at the VA proved to me how much I missed working and how helping people was my passion.

He even holds still long enough for me to get a picture of him.

But, the time comes when he has to go.

"I have to get going, need to get at least a little sleep," he says it on a sigh, and I feel bad for keeping him up, but also touched that he took time to Skype me.

"Go get some sleep, handsome."

At that comment, his lips tip up in a sleepy smile, all for me.

So I do something for once without completely overthinking it.

I bring my fingertips to my lips, kiss them and then blow them at the computer screen. He catches it in his fist and brings it over his chest where he flattens his hand, pressing my kiss right into his heart.

Cue all the melts.

"Be seeing you, sweet girl."

He smiles at me one last time, absolutely wrecking me, and then signs off.

God what just happened.

I have never felt like that just by seeing someone.

I mean Garrett was handsome, but even compared to my husband, Raiden is so...so much more.

I feel a twinge of sadness for thinking these thoughts, but quickly push them down. I'm allowed to feel like this, I'm allowed to think Raid is gorgeous.

This is the new me and the new me is awesome, this is going to take some time but this feels like the direction I am supposed to be heading.

I flop back on my bed, looking once again at the glow in the dark stars on my ceiling. I let out a deep happy breath. My cheeks hurt from smiling so much, just talking to Raiden can change my whole day.

I still can't believe I blew him a kiss… and him pressing it to his heart, ugh, I just about died.

I pull out my phone and look at the picture I took of him, setting it as my background, glad that I'll have a piece of him to carry around with me.

Lost in my daydreams, I feel a cold nose against my temple, about startling me half to death. "Okay baby girl, let's get you outside for a walk, huh?"

Dahlia leaps off the bed and sprints down the stairs. I trail behind her, still unable to think of anything but a drop dead gorgeous Marine that makes my entire heart soar.

Chapter 17

~Raiden~

I'm dreaming of her, and it's the sweetest dream. She's walking toward me, her mile-long legs carrying her easily my way.

Her California tan making her Scandinavian skin glow like radiant moonlight.

Her long blonde hair in waves down her back, some making its way into her eyes, she pushes it back, looking up at me with her glacial blue eyes, so beautiful.

She reaches me and wraps her arms around my waist, chin on my chest looking up at me like I'm the only man in the world. Until this moment, I never knew I wanted to feel like this, but having her look at me like that makes me want to hold onto this feeling forever.

I hold her close for a few minutes, relishing the feeling of having her against me. Then I bring my hands up lightly trailing up her back, over her bare shoulders that are all but begging me to have a taste.

I lean down, unable to resist and start peppering her sun kissed skin with kisses, my lips finding their way closer to her neck, up it, as she leans to give me better access, her breaths coming out in rapid puffs.

I finally get to her jaw and leave a trail of searing kisses there as well.

Just as I'm getting to her pouty perfect lips, amazed at how badly I want this beautiful woman, I hear something, off in the distance.

"Ffffffffffuck, NO, NO BACK OFF!"

I look down at Elli, my sweet girl, who is just as confused as I am at this commotion somewhere in the background.

"AHHHHH NO, NO, GET AWAY."

I whip around, losing the grip I had on my girl, trying to find whatever is making the noise.

I turn around to look for her and she's saying something but I can't hear it, I can barely make out her lips mouthing, "Weston, help Weston."

It's then that I wake up, bolt upright and lock eyes on Weston's thrashing body.

I leap off of my cot and skid over to him, a hand going to his shoulder.

"Motherfucker, get off me! I'll kill you! I'll kill you before you kill me!"

His screams are wracking his whole body, his breathing hard and heavy, he's practically hyperventilating.

"WESTON, WAKE UP!"

I yell, shaking his shoulder and pinning him to his cot.

His eyes snap open and he looks around disoriented. "What happened, Raiden?"

He goes to grip my wrist, probably trying to move me off him but just holds on, and I can feel him shaking.

"You were having a nightmare, man."

His ragged bloodshot eyes look up at me, still gripping my wrist, and I can all but feel the fear, the anguish coming off him in waves. Like a sonic blast, I'm hit with all the emotion swirling in from his nightmare.

"You good, man? I'm worried about you," I say, tightening my hold on his shoulder a little, letting him know I'm here, I'm real and I am really worried about him.

"Yeah man, I'm good, I just get these memories coming at me in my dreams every now and then and it kinda wrecks me."

He releases me and relaxes back on his pillow.

I look at him pointedly. "You need help sortin' that shit out, you come to me, West. I might not be able to help get rid of 'em but I can at least listen to what's going on."

I back up toward my own cot.

"Thanks, brother. Don't know what I would do without you."

He rolls over ending the conversation and on that, I sit down, the adrenaline fading I find myself suddenly mourning the loss of dream-Elli in my arms, and sure as hell worried about my best friend, my brother. Leaning back, I check my watch seeing we only have about an hour until we have to be up and facing another day in this sandy hell.

I don't know what's going on with Weston but I know he won't see anyone about it, he's just too stubborn. I can only hope that he can talk to me about it and maybe getting it out will help it stop weighing on his subconscious. He would do the same for me and it's honestly the least I can do for him. I don't want to push him and I don't truly know how to deal with this.

I bring my hands behind my head and close my eyes trying to coax the woman of my dreams back to me.

Ahhhh, there she is.

I see her, everything else fading to a dull haze, my focus solely on her.

She's walking toward me again, coming to rest in my arms.

She places a hand on my chest, smiling up at me, a smile so bright it's lighting up my whole world.

I bring my hand up to cover hers, my eyes locked on hers, my oceans staring into her glaciers. I run my callused fingers across the backs of her feminine soft ones and come to rest on a ring.

I look down to see what hand is on my chest and realize that it's her left hand, and the ring I was just feeling is an engagement ring.

Not just any engagement ring, but my mother's.

She also has a slim platinum band nestled next to it.

She tilts her head and takes the hand I'm using to explore hers with and intertwines them together.

It's just then that I realize on my left hand is a simple platinum band as well.

I open my eyes, the sunrise filtering through the mouth of our tent casting the ceiling in shadows. I rub my eyes, not fully understanding what's going on in my head at this current moment.

Marriage.

Mama's ring.

Elli.

I've never really wanted to settle down or gave it any thought, but that just felt incredible. I mean, I can't even begin to describe the feeling of content happiness that I had, looking down and seeing Elli, my wife's hand in mine with both of our wedding rings.

I shake my head, pushing the sense of longing I have for that feeling back so I can go out and face the day.

Chapter 18

~Elli~

"Hey thanks, Elli! We'll see ya next week!" Annette the lovely front desk clerk hollers at me as I head through the front doors of the VA. I wave back at her, excited and anxious to get home.

It's been a hell of a long week and I just want to settle down with my puppy, my Kindle and a bottle of wine.

I pull Eleanor - my gunmetal grey Mustang- into the driveway and shut her down. Pausing to release a long gust of air I didn't realize I was holding in. I feel like I probably held it in all week, I'm just so drained.

Going back to work has truly brought me purpose again, something I didn't know I so desperately needed.

When you feel broken, I guess it's easy to push everyone out and let yourself wallow in your grief. Slowly but surely I'm realizing living like a zombie isn't something that was working anymore.

It only took one step, *one email,* and it set me down a path to bring myself back.

I grab my backpack and purse, lock my car and walk into my house. "Dahlia baby, Mama's home!" I barely get my greeting out before my furry roommate barrels into my legs.

I bend down, dropping my bags and give her some kisses and pets. I never get tired of seeing how happy she is when I come home. It makes me feel needed and I crave that feeling. In addition to feeling needed and depended on, I find myself yearning to be desired, and yearning with desire myself.

Skyping Raiden was, to put it mildly, incredible.

I loved being able to see his handsome face. It was like coming home after a long trip, like my heart suddenly flushed with feeling once again.

Queuing up my phone, I look at him as my background, a smile playing at the corners of my lips. I caught him in a sexy little half smirk that if I'm being totally honest here, made me so wet I almost couldn't stand it. I'm not sure if he saw, but I had to press my thighs together so tight to stop me from coming undone right there on the spot.

I set Raiden aside and go to take a shower, relaxation the only thing on my mind. The water is hot and welcome, soothing the muscles I didn't realize were aching.

With the water rushing over my head, my thoughts turn back to Raiden.

How can someone so far away make me feel like this.

I've never met him and yet I feel like I know him, and in turn want to know everything there is about him. Learning little pieces of his life is like watching your favorite primetime show each week. I tune in happy to learn and excited to uncover more.

And God is he handsome.

I really wasn't kidding when I told him he was "to die for." The more I see of him, the more I like.

With how sculpted his arms are I can only imagine how mouthwatering the rest of his body is.

Strong broad chest, defined abs, maybe even that amazing V that only really shredded guys have.

Ughhhhh.

Swoon.

Just the thought of him and his body makes my body tingle with awareness.

My hands trail down my breasts lightly brushing my nipples, with thoughts of how hard Raid's body is, how it would feel against mine, just skin to skin.

I shake myself out of these less than decent thoughts and breathe heavily.

Good lord, that man's body does something to me.

For two whole years, I haven't done anything like that.

Nothing past taking a normal non-sexual shower and getting dressed.

No battery operated boyfriend or anything. Okay, that's a lie… I do have a B.O.B but I don't use him that much. Basically, no orgasms for two whole years.

Now all I can think about is how many orgasms in a row Raid could give me.

Which as delicious as that sounds, makes me feel bad. Definitely not as bad as I would have felt a few weeks ago but definitely makes me feel the loss of my husband and more acutely the loss of myself.

I metaphorically threw myself over a cliff of grief when he died that I'm realizing just how much I missed out on. I'm only twenty-six, I have so much I can still do.

So, once again I have to remind myself that I am allowed to feel happy, I am allowed to feel excited, I am probably maybe just a little bit allowed to lust after the hard body I'm becoming more and more infatuated with.

I shut off the tap and step out to dry off, slipping into my standard comfy hoodie and shorts. I make my way down the stairs and pad to the kitchen to grab a bottle of my favorite Moscato.

Settling into the couch with Dahlia making herself comfortable on my feet, I open up my Kindle, wanting to get lost in the tumultuous world of hot bikers and their old ladies.

After half a bottle of wine to myself I must have dozed off because I'm suddenly not in my house anymore with a sleeping pile of fur on my legs.

I'm somewhere warm and light and Raiden is here.

I'm walking toward him, so very happy to be doing so.

He's standing there waiting for me, so I go to him and wrap my arms around his waist. He feels so hard and so right, up against me, it feels so incredible to be held by him.

Then he's kissing my shoulder, and my neck, and my jaw.

I feel like I'm going to melt into a puddle right at his feet if he keeps going.

I bring my hand up to his chest, loving how I can feel every muscle beneath his black T-shirt.

He then runs his hard working man's hand across mine and stops when he feels the ring on my finger.

A ring I hadn't noticed until just now.

Except this isn't my engagement ring from Garrett, and it isn't the wedding band he put on my finger.

The engagement ring is a breathtaking vintage set, taller than my previous one and perfect next to the slim platinum wedding band resting near it.

He's looking down at it with the same wonderment I am.

So I take his hand in mine, lacing our fingers to reveal to us both an identical platinum band on his ring finger.

Our eyes meet then, and a white-hot electric current pulses through me.

His eyes seem to crackle with energy and passion, which I am swept away in the instant his lips meet mine.

He gives me a bruising heated kiss with enough passion to overdose on.

I want more.

I need more.

His hands hard against my back, crushing my body against his.

He runs them down until they're resting under my ass and lifts me up, where my only choice is to wrap my legs around his waist.

He's devouring my mouth with his, giving me pleasure beyond anything I've ever experienced and it's only a kiss. I lean back and bite my lip, feeling how swollen it is from his heated touch.

Still holding tight with my thighs I lean back to get his shirt off, all but ripping it from his body. What's underneath has me almost drooling, his taught abs, defined chest and so much ink I can't even see it all.

He grinds up against me, right where I need him to be and I'm panting, needing him so badly I can't even see straight. I start writhing against him, needing just a little more friction to get where I need so very badly to be.

And then...I wake up.

Fuck. Seriously?

I blink, trying to slow my racing heart and tamp down the unbridled need coursing through my veins.

I look at my phone and it's a little before midnight. I close my eyes tight, letting out a frustrated breath, willing myself to calm down.

I haven't been that worked up in ages, and damn I was *so* close. The echoes of a phantom orgasm just there beyond my reach.

Chapter 19

~Raiden~

We've been in the desert for almost twenty-four hours.

And it fucking blows.

This is the worst part of being out here, besides the elements, it's the waiting, the staking out.

Base got wind of an insurgent camp out here and we are here to neutralize the threat. Take 'em out before they take us out.

I didn't get into the Marines to kill people, that was never it for me. It wasn't even my intent to take this route, become Special Ops.

My dad was, and yeah I got in in the beginning for the legacy, live up to what dear old dad did for our country.

But then the Marines saw potential in me and I fell in love with protecting people.

I fell in love with the comradery and the teamwork. My brothers mean everything to me, and up till now, I couldn't really see myself on any other path.

Now, sitting out here waiting for the shit to get real, I can't help but wonder what my next step could be.

This being my third tour, I think I'm getting worn out.

I'm consistently impatient and tired.

I just don't have the fire I used to getting into the deep shit.

Part of me also wonders if this is Eli's influence on me. That maybe because she's letting me get close, I want to get closer. I can't get closer when I'm this far away.

I stretch my legs out in front of me, trying to relieve some of the tension.

What kind of job would I be good at when I've spent the last ten years with a gun in my hand, going places only the best of the best do?

I still think I'll want to do something where I can protect people, maybe even use a gun in some other way, on a smaller scale.

I'm daydreaming about my possible future career when Weston nudges me.

"Hey man, talk to me I'm falling asleep out here."

He yawns, which only furthers his point.

"What do you want me to talk about, buddy?"

I turn his way, scanning beyond him looking toward the non-activity that's happening. "Why don't you tell me about this girl you carry around in your pocket?"

My hand instinctively goes to the pocket I keep Eli tucked away in.

I bring it out so he can look at her and smirk when he whistles.

"She's a beauty, brother."

I take her back and stare down, feeling her melt right into my heart.

"Yeah, she's breathtaking isn't she."

Weston just looks at me with an amused expression.

"Why you looking at me like that, West?"

He cocks an eyebrow and smirks at me.

"Oh, just happy you are finally feeling what it's like to be in love."

My eyes widen and I lean over to punch him in the arm.

"Hey now, no one ever said I was in love with her."

I shake my head and tuck Elli safely back in my pocket.

"You didn't have to say anything, I can tell. You all but sprint into the comm tent every chance you get, you wake up fucking happy and you've been sayin' her name in your sleep lately."

He winks at me and I know I'm red faced.

I had no idea I'd been saying her name in my sleep, it makes sense though. It just brings back the sweet memory of having my wife's hand in mine, her body pressed up against me. Weston is still looking at me, smug as shit.

Could I be in love with someone I've never met?

He leaves me to my thoughts and turns back to the scene in front of us, still ripe with non-activity.

My thoughts are centered on Eli, her smile, her eyes, her laugh. The way she says my name when she asked to take a picture of me so she could keep a piece of me with her.

My fist goes up to rub my chest, right over my heart.

I've never been in love before, just had fun fucking my way through my downtime between deployments.

Sure, I want to fuck Elli more than I want to breathe.

Just seeing her long tan legs through the computer made me want to find out what it's like when they're wrapped around my waist while I'm rocking into her.

I have to reach down and adjust myself, these thoughts taking a very naughty turn. Honestly, thinking about it, the more I learn about her, her passion, her drive, it just makes me want to know more.

I want to know her fears, her dreams, what makes her happy.

How I can make her happy.

Keep that laugh I love so much ringing in my ears.

I don't know if this is love but I know this is different than anything I've felt for anyone. Which only brings me back to thoughts of a life outside of the Marines.

Outside of the war.

I sigh.

Only about three and a half months left and we'll be coming home.

I'll be able to see my sweet girl.

God, I hope she wants to see me.

Chapter 20

~Elli~

I check my phone for probably about the fiftieth time today just to see my Raiden.

Huh, my Raiden.

Never thought of it like that before. But I like how that sounds, I'm his sweet girl and he's my Raid.

My heart beats a little quicker and I'm starting to blush, which is a little mortifying considering I'm in lulu lemon and the girls are looking at me like I'm a loony bird.

I working on calming myself down and purchase my new yoga pants, spendy for sure, but nothing beats quality and now, I have some extra money to blow.

The VA gave me a bonus because I refuse to let them pay me over minimum wage and this was the only way they could show how much they value me.

I tried to give it back, but no one would hear anything about it.

So, here I am spending a little on myself and actually really enjoying it.

Treat yo self, right?

I unlock my car and slide down into her and rev her up, loving how she sounds. Which of course takes me to another thought of Raiden.

I'm coming to realize the more I talk to him, the more I invest in 'this' whatever 'this' is between us, everything makes me think of him.

For once, it's a nice reprieve from thinking about Garrett.

I drive home, blasting some old school hip-hop, totally jamming out.

Right as I'm pulling up in front of my house my phone dings with an email notification.

I snatch it up quick and have to swipe the screen five times before I finally get it open because I'm so giddy.

To: norwegianbeauty@gmail.com
From: usmcraider1@gmail.com
Subject: Home

Sweet girl,

What do you think of me getting out of the service?
When I come off tour, I was thinking of changing my path a bit, maybe tweaking it.
This has been my path for so long and I just don't know that I want it to be the only path I take my entire life.

I miss you, Elli. I hope you're doing okay over there, so far away from me.

Only a little while till I can come home, will you want to meet me?

Will you go to dinner with me?

Sorry for the twenty questions, haha.

I am just so damn tired. Tired of being over here. Tired of not being able to hear your voice when I want to.

Tell me when I can call you.

I need to hear my sweet girl's voice.

-Raiden

My heart is stuttering in my chest.

There's blood rushing in my ears and I'm tearing up a little bit.

Raiden wants to see *me*.

He wants to take me out to dinner.

Oh God, I want that so much.

He's crazy if he thinks I won't fucking jump on the chance to spend time with him when he comes home.

I have to see him.

Period.

I tap out my response, hoping he's around and not busy so he can talk to me more, because…. I miss him too.

To: usmcraider1@gmail.com
From: norwegianbeauty@gmail.com
Subject: RE: Home

Hi Handsome,

YES.

And I think if you want to get out, you should do it.
I am becoming a firm believer in going for your goals, living your dreams.
I forgot how much I loved being a paramedic, being able to help people and I never want to lose that again.
Helping people, saving them, it brings me so much happiness I can barely stand it.
If you want to change careers, you do it, sweetheart.
I miss you too, Raid.
More than I probably have a right to... Boy, is that scary to admit.
Call me whenever you can and I'll answer.
I promise I will even if it's late at night, early in the morning, at work, whenever.
I'll be here.

-Your sweet girl

I hit send and exhale.
His sweet girl.

I'm wrapped up in the bliss of Raiden, and I come to the conclusion I've been his for a while.

I remember when Garrett and I met, it wasn't love at first sight.

We had to work on it, but we did make it and we loved each other hard.

With Raiden, this feeling is absolutely *effortless*.

Like falling through the sky, my heart just completely soars when I get to talk to him, get to see him, hear his deep bourbon voice.

Loving Raiden is so easy.

I stop.

Love.

Raiden.

Love.

My chest rises and falls at the realization that I'm not only Raiden's sweet girl...I'm also falling in love with him.

I stare down at my hands and see them trembling, I know why...it's because I'm scared.

I am one hundred percent scared to death.

What if this doesn't work out and 'this' between us ends?

It's barely even begun, and I know already if I lost Raiden I would never recover, going through that kind of loss twice? Unthinkable.

I lean back into the headrest and let my eyes wander, my mind racing, bringing back thoughts of my dream once more.

Raiden and I, *married*.

A smile tickles my lips and the fear is replaced by hope. A feeling that became so damned unfamiliar that at first I don't recognize it.

My smile gets bigger, a giggle escaping my dry throat.

Hope, I have hope.

I snap a selfie and attach it to a new email.

To: usmcraider1@gmail.com
From: norwegianbeauty@gmail.com
Subject: Hope
Attachment: elli.jpeg

Raiden,

I wanted you to know I'm wearing the smile you gave me.

Love,
Elli

I had pinned that quote on Pinterest and I thought it would be cute to let him know I feel something... something strong.

But I also want to test the waters and see if he's falling for me the way I'm falling for him.

I sigh, a happy breath that lets all the anxiety ebb away from me.

I finally slide out of Eleanor and head inside to give the puppy some loving, the sweet feelings left over from Raiden's email still wrapping me up tight.

Chapter 21

~Raiden~

"*I'm wearing the smile you gave me...Love, Elli*".
Sweet girl...what are you doing to me?

I print her picture and tuck it away with the other one, getting more and more worn, I can't seem to not look at it at least fifty times a day.

I step out of the comm tent and almost run straight into Weston who is bouncing from one foot to the other.

"Whoa dude, what are you doing? Spying on me or some shit?"

I poke him in the chest playfully because of course, I know my brother wouldn't invade my privacy but it's still fun to take the piss out on him.

"Guess what, man! Guess fucking what!"

He grabs my shoulders shaking me back and forth like a rag doll. I grab his forearms to steady myself and say, "What?!" He is so excited, I don't think I've ever seen him like this, it's absolutely hilarious!

"They're pulling us out early."

Did I actually hear him correctly? I can feel my eyes get big and I just stare, not moving, not breathing.

Weston chuckles and starts waving a hand in front of my eyes, trying to break me out of my trance. I slowly blink, bringing him back into focus and finally take a breath.

I choke out, "We.... we're going home?" My throat suddenly so dry I'm surprised I even spoke.

Weston busts up laughing, smacking me right in the face with his happiness it's radiating off him in waves.

"Yeah buddy, we're going home the end of next week!"

He shakes me a little and then turns me around back in the comm tent, where he forces me to sit down, while I'm still in a daze. He bends down next to me and forces me to look at him.

"Skype your girl, call her, email her, whatever the hell you two do, and tell her the good news man."

On that, he walks out and I just sit there with my hands in my lap.

Elli.

I can meet her.

I can change my path.

I can find new dreams.

It's all becoming so real. My sweet fantasy suddenly becoming reality.

I shake my head bringing me out of my delirious thoughts and crack the biggest fucking smile the world has ever seen.

I bring up my email, and then shut it back down, needing to see her beautiful face when I tell her the news.

I click to open Skype, praying she's online. Which, as if she can sense that I need to talk to her right now, she is.

Before I can even click to connect to her, an accept call comes through from her.

Duh, accept.

My sweet beautiful girl fills up the computer screen, looking absolutely delectable. Her hair cascading around her shoulders, no makeup, glasses on, a big T-shirt and yoga pants on. Sexiest creature alive.

She throws me a blinding smile while I just stare at her, caught up in how perfect she is. "Elli, babe, I'm coming home."

I let it slip out, a smirk tipping up my lips.

She pauses looking dumbfounded for a second, only a second, and then her squeal fills the entire comm tent.

"ARE YOU SERIOUS?!"

Her hands fly up to her mouth to stifle her screeching and if I'm not mistaken I can see her eyes start to well up with tears. I lean in closer to the web cam.

"Yeah, end of next week, I'm coming home." My voice is really husky at her reaction.

I see a tear break free and roll down her cheek, then stopping at her hand, still covering her mouth, my eyes watching its descent.

"Sweet girl, why are you crying?"

A note of concern peaks through my voice.

"Raid," she breathes, "I am so happy."

More tears fall and then it hits me that she's crying because she's happy I'm coming home.

She cares that much.

My heart bursts like a dozen fireworks in my chest, seeing my girl crying with joy for me. I've never had anyone care about me like this. I can see it in her eyes, she feels like I do. This beautiful, fragile yet strong woman feels like I do...

Breaking me free of my thoughts she asks ever so timidly, "Can I come meet you when you get in.... like at the base?"

She wants to meet me the second my boots hit American soil... Fuck me.

"Yes baby, please meet me, I need to see you."

She blushes a deep scarlet when I call her baby, and God If I don't cherish that blush. This girl...

"Email me the details and I'll be there, handsome."

She gives me a shy smile once more and I know it then, I'm a goner.

She's gonna have me wrapped around her little finger the second I see her, hell, I already am and we aren't anywhere near each other.

We talk for an hour, basking in the intoxicating bliss of being able to connect even if it's just through the internet.

When I finally have to peel myself away this time, I blow her a kiss and tell her I'll be seeing her soon.

My heart so full to the brim, I almost can't walk. This next week better fly by because I need to feel Elli in my arms, knowing how it felt in my dreams I just know the real thing is going to take my breath away.

Chapter 22

~Elli~

"I think you should wear this."

Jen holds up a slinky yellow sundress, I just eyeball it, and sigh.

"It's no use girl, I have no idea what to wear."

I flop back on my bed, Dahlia rolling over to snuggle into my side. I stare up at the ceiling, desperate. My best friend lies down beside me and stares into the space with me. "Girlfriend, you've got it bad."

I turn to her and narrow my eyes.

"Oh I do not. I just don't know what to wear!" I huff out. "He hasn't met me in person and the only time he's seen me is in my comfy clothes." I scowl, and she busts up laughing. "I can't even believe my ears! You haven't given one single thought to your wardrobe in I don't know how long, especially not for some guy." She looks at me, thoroughly amused at my dismay over an outfit.

"Jennifer, you just don't get it!" I growl. "I have to look like a goddess when he sees me, it's just…it's important to me okay?"

She gives me one last look, one that has me questioning what she's thinking when she startles both my dog and me when she jumps off the bed. She goes to my closet and comes out a few minutes later with my black Flying Monkey skinnies, a lavender flowing tank from Free People and my Frye wedges.

I smirk, seeing she has found exactly what would indeed make me look like a goddess. "Jen, you are a miracle worker." She takes a bow and giggles, happy she could dress me, one of her favorite things to do.

"Now, put this on so we can get you on the road. The sooner you get there, the sooner I can get all the juicy details." She winks and walks out of the room, Dahlia hot on her heels hoping for treats, no doubt.

I get dressed, shaking out my loose curls and assess the total package.

The jeans definitely accentuate my booty and my calves, two of my favorite assets. The tank is perfect because it shows off cleavage but not enough to be deemed inappropriate.

I take one last look at myself, pleased with the effect and walk out into the kitchen. Jen is leaning up against the counter smirking.

"What?" I eye her suspiciously.

"You look hot, mama."

I laugh, "Thanks, babe."

I grab my keys, purse and phone, and we both head out the door, leaving my grumpy puppy behind.

"Okay, text me when you get there and then text me whenever you can, I am itching to know how it goes."

She pauses, then looks at me, hope shining in her eyes. "I'm so glad I have my best friend back, please let me meet him sometime so I can thank him..." She leans in for a tight hug then spins me toward Eleanor and smacks my ass.

I blow her a kiss and hop in, nervousness settling in the pit of my stomach.

I'm finally going to meet him.

Finally really only being after three and a half months, but it truly feels like forever.

I adjust my rearview mirror, catching my reflection. I take in this girl, so different from the person she was only a short time ago. My eyes brighter. My heart lighter. My spirit more free than it has been in so long.

I take a beat to close my eyes and remind myself that I can do this.

I'm moving forward, bit-by-bit.

Raiden isn't the sole reason for me changing, but he truly was the catalyst. From the very first email, he listened to me. He didn't try to fix me or give me advice beyond telling me not to poke at my broken pieces. He understood what I needed without even knowing me. The more I talked to him the more I realized how lonely I had been, and even then I had no idea he would mean this much to me...

And today I get to meet him.

I start my car and back out of the driveway.

I'm so ready to drive into my future it isn't even funny.

Chapter 23

~Raiden~

"You nervous?" Weston speaks somewhere to the left of me.

I've been rubbing my hands together for the last ten minutes as the plane started making its descent from the sky.

"Ah, I don't know. Kind of?"

I look over at him, feeling honestly like a little bitch.

His deep laughter fills my ears. "Dude, you got this."

I look back down at my lap, my throat slightly parched.

"Yeah, I just can't wait to see her."

He leans into me. "Happy for you, brother." He claps me on the back.

I take a minute to get ahold of myself. We'll be landing in a few and I need to pull it together.

Elli, sweet girl.

This whole past week had been some sort of fresh hell.

The need to come home only adding to my anxiety level. I don't know how I would have made it another month and a half over there being away from her.

The plane's wheels touch down, my body rocking at the slight impact, my head whips up and to the side to see Weston smirking at me, knowing I might possibly be meeting my future in a few minutes.

The whole platoon stands up in unison, brothers in arms, ready to see their families. I swallow my nervousness and move forward, Weston right behind me.

The air hits me and I feel home. The sweet smell of eucalyptus trees teasing my already tightly strung senses. The slight breeze blowing through my now longer than regulation hair. We file out of the plane and onto the tarmac. The sun kisses my skin, a completely different feeling than feeling the sun in Iraq.

I'm home.

There is no place on earth like California.

We stay in formation to be saluted by the higher ups and then we break apart, little kids running to their parents, their significant others in tears at their arrival, safe. Deployments are hard on them, no doubt about that and it warms my heart knowing that my brothers can be home and with their person.

Which really only serves to ramp up my excitement to see *my* person.

I walk toward the gate where I asked Elli to meet me, my heart starting to race.

As I near our spot my heart completely stops, my mouth going bone dry.

She's standing there in black skinny jeans, a purple top, her hair curly and flowing around her shoulders like soft silk. She has her hands in front of her, and it looks like she's rubbing them together nervously, identical to me only moments ago.

She looks up.

She sees me standing there barely a yard away, staring at her beauty.

Her hands drop away and she takes a cautious step toward me.

So I take one too.

Then, as if throwing whatever caution there was to the wind, she runs toward me, slamming into me with enough force to knock me back, her toned arms going around my neck.

I drop my duffel, picking her up and crushing her to me, burying my face in her neck, breathing her in.

She smells of lilies, just like the ones in my mama's garden.

A feeling of being absolutely complete takes me over and I whisper, "Elli," my voice rasping with emotion.

I feel her start to shake, and I lean back slightly so I can see her beautiful face.

She has tears dripping from her eyelashes falling onto her sun-kissed cheeks.

I set her down and use the pads of my thumbs to wipe them away, ever so gently, feeling like a giant brute with my hands on this tiny pixie of a woman.

"Don't cry, beautiful."

She looks up at me, tearing my soul in shreds seeing those tears in her eyes.

She breathes out a soft "Raid" and buries her face in my chest, overcome with emotion.

My arms go to wrap around her, already feeling that this is where she belongs, in my arms, with me.

I kiss the top of her head and hold her there, happy to do so forever if she would let me. I don't think I have ever in my life felt the way like I do with Elli in my arms.

Like I would do anything and everything to protect her, to make her happy, keep her smiling.

I let my lips linger on her hair.

How have I gone this long not feeling a fraction of the emotion I feel for this woman?

Weston coughs once behind me, breaking the spell we're wrapped in.

Eli leans back and we both turn, she wipes her eyes and I tuck her into my side, a protective arm around her.

"So this is her, huh?" he inquires, smiling. "I'm Weston, your boy here's best friend."

Elli clears her throat and steps toward him, surprising both of us when she goes up on her tiptoes to give him a tight hug.

"Thank you for your service, Weston."

He clears his own throat, looking at me from over her shoulder, surprised as hell, and pats her back gently.

"Of course."

She steps back and stands between us, my girl and my best friend.

"Well," stepping back, "you two probably want some time alone, I'm gonna head home to my bachelor pad." I laugh, knowing just how much of a bachelor he really is.

At that, Weston turns, giving me a nod and walking away.

Elli turns toward, me, seemingly shy but radiating energy.

"I'm so glad you're here, Raiden."

I exhale, my heart so full, my soul feeling so free.

"I'm glad too sweet girl."

She steps closer once more to give me another hug, her arms going around my waist. "What do you want to do now that you're back stateside?" she asks, her ear over my heart.

I laugh. "I could really go for some In-N-Out, a burger sounds like heaven." She lets out a loud laugh, the sound tinkling in my ears, sending me soaring.

"Come on then. Let's get out of here."

She smiles up at me and I grab her hand, lacing our fingers together.

I'm *home.*

Chapter 24

~Elli~

I feel so safe.

I feel so protected.

So surrounded.

So…happy.

I didn't know I could experience a feeling like this again, but here I am…in Raid's arms and in this moment I know there is no better place to be.

I was so very nervous when I saw his plane land. I thought I was going to break my hands, I was wringing them so hard.

Then it intensified to a full on body sweat, goose bumps and everything when his platoon came down the tarmac.

It brought back a rush of memories of waiting for Garrett to come home.

But to be honest, I know this is different, it doesn't feel familiar past the fact I've done this same song and dance before.

This time I'm not waiting for my husband to come home.

This time I'm waiting for someone I've never met. I'm waiting for... him.

I was so busy overthinking everything that I didn't see him walking toward me until he was just...right there.

I looked up and there he was.

Like a dark angel materializing right in front of me.

I caught his eyes and saw nothing but blue fire behind them, a heat that drew me toward him like a magnetic field.

A moth drawn to the flame.

When he took a step toward me, I couldn't take being patient. Like I had done it every day before, I ran straight to him, no inhibition, and no fear.

Just him.

I slammed into his body knocking him back slightly, but he recovered just as fast and then was crushing me against his hard body.

A bliss so intense engulfed me and I thought I might drown in happiness until he whispered "Elli" ever so softly in his deep bourbon voice. I thought I was drowning in bliss before...this was a full on tsunami of emotion.

So I did what every rational sane woman would do in the arms of a man she has only just met...start crying.

Thank the Lord I put on the waterproof this morning because at the point I couldn't stop. He loosened his grip and looked down at me, concern shining deep from behind those blue eyes.

Concern for me.

He cupped my face in his big hands and wiped away my tears, being so very delicate with me.

"Don't cry, beautiful."

His smile, his eyes, so beautiful...swoon.

I can't do anything but whisper his name and bury my face back in his chest.

My new favorite place.

I feel his lips on my hair and all I can think is how very much I want to feel those lips. It's almost overwhelming how badly I want to know what he tastes like.

I hear a cough behind us and step back, but I don't get very far because already, Raiden is pulling me into his side.

A man I'm guessing has to be Weston is standing there close to us.

He's built like Raid, covered in thick muscles and tanned tattooed skin, so similar to the man holding me close that you could mistake them for brothers.

The greatest difference between them is where Raiden is all dark hair and blue eyes, Weston is all dark hair and grey eyes, and you can barely tell he's older but a few grey hairs by his ears give him away.

"So this is her, huh?"

Oh, Raiden talks about me?

"I'm your boy here's best friend, Weston."

Knew it.

I know I surprise both of them when I step over to Weston and embrace him in a hug, thanking him for his service. What I wanted to say was thank you for keeping my guy safe, but beyond that I wanted him to know just how appreciated his sacrifices are to a civilian.

He pats my back awkwardly and I step back, closer to the arms I'm already missing. Weston says he's going to go home to his bachelor pad, which makes me laugh along with my guy, leaving me along with Raiden once more.

I still can't wrap my head or my heart around the fact Raiden is actually here, standing in front of me.

I don't feel awkward, I feel like this is someone I know, someone I've spent time with, know intimate things about, and someone I've loved.

It's relaxing and overwhelming both at once.

All I want to do is stand here in his arms, but I know we should get out of here.

I ask him what he wants to do now that he's home, and he replies, "I could really go for some In-N-Out, a burger sounds like heaven."

Who am I to deny this soldier a burger?

He's staring at me.

Because I feel so comfortable around him, I didn't really stop to rein in my devouring of this burger. I must look like some sort of uncivilized cave person.

I set the double-double down in the basket and wipe my face with my napkin.

"What are you staring at?" I ask, my voice quiet.

He laughs. A sound that reverberates straight into my chest, so deep and strong.

"I'm staring at you, babe."

I narrow my eyes, feeling slightly embarrassed yet still playful.

"But why?"

He smirks.

Ugh.

Why does he have to do that? It's completely unfair how sexy it is.

"Two reasons." He's still smirking, holding up two fingers.

"One, it's sexy how much you're enjoying that burger. Don't ask me why, it just is. Two, you're gorgeous."

"Oh."

He laughs. "Oh," copying me.

I can tell I'm blushing, my cheeks heating up.

He winks at me and goes back to finishing his own double-double.

Now it's my turn to stare. I take full advantage of his concentration on eating and absolutely devour his looks.

So handsome.

So rugged.

His hair is longer than I've seen it on the webcam and I like it. It looks soft like if I ran my fingers through it, I would be running them through silk.

His eyes are still trained down at his food so I can marvel at how long his eyelashes are. You wouldn't think long eyelashes on a guy is sexy, but on Raiden, it's beyond gorgeous. It makes his blue eyes pop even more than they already do.

Lost in thoughts of how unbelievably handsome he is, I don't notice him look up and catch me staring at him. He raises an eyebrow and I quickly move my eyes away, trying to act nonchalant but knowing I've been caught red handed.

"Hey, wanna get out of here?" His voice is so deep and smooth pulling my eyes back to his.

I let out an excited breath.

"Yeah, what do you have in mind?"

He reaches up and scratches his jaw, the stubble making a rough sound.

"Let me drive? I want to take you somewhere."

I reach into my purse and hand over my keys without giving it a second thought.

No one drives my car but me. I don't even like taking it to the dealership. But something about Raiden makes me want to trust him...with everything.

My hands almost moved of their own accord when he asked. He brushes his fingers against my palm ever so slightly, sparks of electricity shooting up my arm.

Our eyes lock, crackling with energy of their own, our breaths coming out in short erratic puffs.

I don't stop feeling the electric current pulsing through my body when we pull away from In-N-Out. It just simmers low, creating a wanton feeling in me, for more.

More electricity.

More small touches.

More.

I play DJ and plug my phone into the stereo.

Putting it on shuffle I let fate decide what the tune will be, when "Something in The Way You Move" by Ellie Goulding starts up, I mentally high five her, go Ellie.

The beat pulses through me, making me want to jam out, so I do.

I move my shoulders and head to the beat, feeling light and free.

Not a care in the world, the first time in what feels like forever.

She sings about strange feelings and it sure does resonate with me.

My cheeks heat up, knowing Raiden heard the words the same way I just did.

She mentions falling in love and oh does that do something for me, with Raiden being so close.

My heart starts beating faster, so I just cover it up by continuing to dance and sing along with her.

In my peripheral, I can see him smirking, amused by the show I'm putting on for him.

I love seeing that smirk.

Chapter 26

~Raiden~

She is without a doubt the cutest fucking thing I have ever seen.

She's dancing to the music and singing a song I hadn't heard before but it seemed to perfectly describe what I was feeling in that moment.

Being in her presence is absolutely intoxicating. I can't seem to take a full deep breath because she keeps stealing it away.

I have never felt like this with a woman, never felt amped up and sated at the same time.

Watching her eat was borderline erotic, the way she was enjoying herself so thoroughly. It made me happy to see she was being relaxed with me because that is exactly how I felt with her. I even told her she was sexy while she was eating, which put the most adorable heat to her cheeks.

So, not wanting this day to end, I asked her if she wanted to get out of there and taking a long shot, asked if I could drive. She didn't hesitate to give me the keys and now here we are, speeding down the highway to my spot.

A spot I always came to think and just unwind when I was home and needed to get away from the normalcy of being in the states.

I put her car in park and I turn to her, a smile already plastered across my face.

"Ready?" Her eyes sparkle back at me, a sight I know I could never get enough of.

God, what is she doing to me?

I'm enthralled.

I get out of her Mustang, a gorgeous car I have to say, whole lotta power too.

She crosses in front of the hood to stand beside me, looking up at my tall frame.

"Where are we, Raiden?"

Her voice, it's like *sex*.

What I would give to hear that voice while I'm inside her.

I clear my throat, definitely letting my mind get away from me.

"This is where I go when I want to get away."

I grab one of her small hands in mine and lace our fingers together, leading her toward the spot.

My boots sink through the sand and it isn't long before she takes her shoes off all together, looping the straps around her other wrist.

It takes us but a minute before we are there and I breathe in the familiar salt air, deep in my lungs.

When I bring us to a stop, she lets out a sharp gasp taking in the view.

We are situated on my favorite stretch of beach between two giant weathered rocks, the sun just starting to go down in the sky.

The effect of the sunset bounces off the waves creating a cascade of different colors crashing toward us.

"Raid, this is breathtaking."

She looks up at me, thanking me with her eyes and I know that is a look I'll spend my life chasing after.

I sit down in the sand and pull her down so she's in between my legs. She hesitates for just a moment before I feel her relax back into me, so I wrap my arms around the front of her shoulders.

Bringing my face down to nuzzle in the back of her neck, breathing her sweet lily smell in. "Elli," I whisper.

She leans back into me further at the sound of me saying her name.

"Yes?" she breathes out.

"Why is this so easy with you?"

She brings her hands up so they rest on my forearms.

"I...don't know Raid," she pauses, "it feels like we've done this a million times, that this isn't the first time we're meeting."

She turns her face slightly, her skin so close to my lips I can almost taste her.

She keeps going, my heart racing, and pulse pounding in my ears.

"It's easy to forget that I'm a widow with you, that you're the first person I've opened up to in over two years." She tightens her grip on me. "You...this...me in your arms, Raid this just feels...natural."

She finishes and her raw beauty entrances me.

She's right.

I couldn't put it into words, didn't know if she felt the same way but she does.

She said it, she feels it, and this isn't just me.

A feeling of hope takes flight in my chest, causing a strangled noise to escape my throat. I hold her tighter against me and she takes it, nestling her sweet little body further into me.

I swear we fit together like we were made for each other.

"Elli," I get out, surprised at my ability to speak at all I'm so awash in emotion.

This is something completely foreign to me, which is probably why I'm not articulating myself very well.

"I've never done this before." I cast my eyes down, unable to keep staring at the sweet skin of her jaw. She runs her fingertips along the muscles in my forearms, making the hair on the back of my neck stand up on end.

She dips her head ever so slowly and kisses where she was just trailing her fingertips. White-hot fire races up my skin, causing my breathing to quicken and my body to tense up.

She whispers, "I *know*, babe."

Fuck, she called me babe.

That's one of the sweetest things I've ever heard, her breath tickling my arms.

She knows, this isn't just me out of my depth here, she's right there with me and that gives me some sense of peace.

We stay like that for at least an hour, her wrapped up tight in my arms. Her body fitting into mine so perfectly. We stay silent, digesting everything happening between us. I think about how only a few days ago I was half a world away dreaming about this incredible woman and now here she is, and I'm experiencing a sensation unlike anything I have ever felt.

My heart feels full, it feels like it's gonna explode and I want it to.

I want the warmth to flood my body and set me on fire, just to feel this way for her.

Chapter 26

~Elli~

I feel his breath tickling across the shell of my ear, and it sends shivers straight down my spine.

I'm surrounded by Raiden.

It's fucking bliss.

We've been quiet for a while but it doesn't feel awkward, it doesn't feel forced or pregnant with unasked questions. It just feels…content and easy.

I breathe in deep, smelling the ocean air, the smell of wet sand and most of all the smell of him.

He isn't wearing any cologne but he smells masculine, clean and salty. The kind of smell I want to roll around in and never stop inhaling because it's so addicting.

This whole time we've been sitting here wrapped up in each other, I haven't thought of Garrett but once.

The one thought that crossed my mind was, how I loved my husband but how this is so much different.

This is so much…more.

Loving Garrett was like learning to ride a bike. Being here with Raid is as easy as if I was made to be in his embrace.

The sun went down a while ago but I don't feel cold at all.

He gives me a tight squeeze that does things to me, a smile breaking out across my face at the feeling.

"Let's get you home, huh?"

Almost on cue, I yawn. I scoot forward so he can get up behind me, then I feel strong arms pull me up from sitting.

He crouches down again and pats his back, I narrow my eyes at him and he laughs. "Come on, you're sleepy."

I huff out a breath, pretending to not be loving this.

I climb on his back like a little monkey and he loops his arms through my legs, holding me safe and secure, giving me a piggyback ride through the sand. My arms are around his neck, my forearms resting on his broad shoulders, I turn my face so I can lay it against the back of his neck, his hair tickling my forehead. I close my eyes and let him carry me back to my car, already missing our intimate moments in the sand.

All too quickly he's setting me down and I'm mourning the feeling of being pressed up against his body.

I look up at him, blue eyes shining so brightly in the darkness.

"Where are you staying?"

He rubs the back of his neck looking a little sheepish.

"My mama's house, it's not too far from here, I can walk."

I let out a snort, quickly clamping a hand over my mouth. A surprised look crosses his face and then he's bending over clutching his stomach he's laughing so hard at me.

"Hey! No, you will not walk and stop laughing at me!"

I start giggling, sleepy and feeling embarrassed at my outburst. He's still doubled over laughing so I push his shoulders, acting defensive but not able to be cranky about it.

"You are going to drive us to your mama's house and then I'll drive home, end of story, Raiden."

I try and fail to act stern with him, putting my hands on my hips and everything.

His laugh is infecting me in the best way.

He straightens up still laughing and then stills. His eyes are piercing through mine, right down into my soul.

"I think I like it when you try to boss me."

He smirks, and I'm a goner. A dreamy smile, one I couldn't control if I wanted to, takes over my face.

Fifteen minutes later we are pulling up to a simple yet incredible ranch style home. The garden is the true show stopper, what has to be at least one hundred different lilies are planted strategically, making the yard vibrant even in the soft moonlight.

I'm still caught up in the beauty of this landscape when I hear him shuffle in his seat. I feel a gentle touch on my cheek, which breaks me out of my flower daze and I turn my eyes to him. He opens his hand and places it against my cheek. I close my eyes again and nuzzle my cheek further into his warm palm. The pad of his thumb running across the top of my cheekbone. I open my eyes and see his blue eyes staring back at me, with an indescribable expression written across his handsome face.

With his voice so low and husky he says my name.

"Elli..."

I place my hand on the back of his, feeling how very big he is compared to me.

"Raid..."

Then he's leaning in, his eyes dipping down to my lips.

Oh, yes, yes please kiss me.

Please.

They part on their own accord, feeling my breath come out in little bursts, my heart hammering in my chest so loud I'm surprised he doesn't hear it too. I lean forward just a little, willing him to kiss me.

His dark bourbon voice so close to me, "Sweet girl, give me your phone."

That surprises me, forcing me to pop my eyes open and he's so close, so very achingly close to my lips, right in my face.

Stuck in the magnetic pull of him being so near me I hand him my phone, never moving away from him.

"Close your eyes," he whispers softly.

So I do.

Then my phone is back in my free hand, my other still holding his big hand to my cheek. I feel a breath against my lips, one that isn't my own and my body heats up in anticipation. Then I feel it, the softest brush of his lips…against my forehead.

I open my eyes and he's already leaning back slowly, a soft smile on his lips.

The same lips that just scorched my skin, just not the skin I was expecting.

He opens the door of my car, walking around swiftly to my side and then he's with me once more, pulling me out of my seat and then I'm where I want to be most… in his arms.

He pulls me in close, holding me tightly against his hard body, his lips brushing ever so softly against the top of my head. The tenderness such a contrast from the feeling of his defined muscles pressed against me. I breathe him in, so masculine, so Raiden.

"I'll be seein' you soon, baby."

His voice crashes over me in the most delicious way.

I lean back and look up at him, showing him the smile I'm wearing because of him.

Only him.

"You have my number now so text me when you get home safe, baby."

He looks down at me with adoration.

"Yes, bossy Raiden."

I giggle, feeling lighter than air.

He leans down and presses his lips ever so softly to my forehead once more and then starts walking backward toward the house, a smirk tipping the corners of his lips up and making his eyes sparkle.

He watches me get into my car, struggle with adjusting the seat back to accommodate my much smaller frame and start her up, backing down the driveway. He stays there until I can no longer see him in my mirror. I don't start feeling sad until I get onto the highway and I'm speeding toward my house.

How can I miss him this much when I've only just met him?

When I finally stumble through my front door a little under an hour later, Dahlia is on me in an instant, no doubt angry I've been gone all day. I let her out and grab my phone, anxious to let him know I made it home and have contact with him again.

I scroll through my contacts and find "Raiden" which I shorten to Raid before I open a message to him.

"I'm home safe, but wishing I was still safe with you instead..."

I'm too tired to pretend this isn't exactly how I'm feeling.

I can't pretend with him, I don't want to hide.

It's the most freeing feeling in the world.

I don't have to hide.

My phone vibrates in my hand almost instantly.

"Good, get some sleep sweet girl."

I smile, already moving toward my bed, my puppy hot on my heels.

"Okay, I'm in bed now."

"Dream of me baby, dream of today."

If he only knew that I do dream of him, that those are my absolute favorite dreams when he's holding me close and kissing me.

I reach up and touch the spot where his lips pressed every so tenderly against my forehead, wishing I knew what it was like to feel those lips on mine.

And with that, I drift off.

A smile still ghosting my lips and my heart feeling so full.

A feeling I haven't gotten used to yet, but one I wouldn't trade for the world.

Chapter 27

~Raiden~

It's already morning?

My body is still so groggy from changing time zones. I don't normally have an issue with time zone changes but I was out late last night with Eli and my body is screaming at me that I need more sleep.

I stretch my arms above my head, working out the kinks in my shoulders.

My hands hit the wall right above my bed.

Ow.

I forgot how short my bed is here at my mama's. I have my own apartment but it's a tradition that when I come off tour I stay at Mama's for at least a week. She likes to dote on me and have her baby back. I can't deny that woman anything, especially when there are home cooked meals involved.

I get up, rubbing my eyes and shuffle into the kitchen where my mama is already making breakfast. The smell of pancakes wafting into my nostrils.

She turns around when she hears me in the doorway and squeals.

"Raiden, baby! I am so glad you're awake; I was just making you your favorite."

She rushes over to hug me, I have to lean down so she can get her slight arms around my neck. She gives me a kiss on the cheek and walks back to her cooking.

"So." She turns slightly to look at me over her shoulder.

I just raise my eyebrows, waiting for me to continue.

"Whose Mustang was that?" she smirks.

I let out a breath and chuckle, knowing she's about to pull a 'mom' and give me the third degree.

"Well…a friend's."

She turns around wiping her hands on a towel and levels my gaze.

"A friend, hmm?"

I look down and rub the back of my neck, feeling sheepish.

"Yeah, Mama, well I mean I just kinda met her but it's a long story."

She turns off the stove, dishing up two plates full of pancakes, eggs, and bacon, and pushing one to me across the island.

"I've got nothing but time, son."

I sigh, there's no fighting her when she wants to know something. Never been able to hide a thing from this tenacious stubborn woman.

"Well…her name is Elli. And she started out as my pen pal."

She just watches me across the island, sipping her coffee and silently willing me to keep going, knowing that isn't everything. Like I said can't hide a thing.

Might as well get this out and over with.

"She's a widow, her husband was a SEAL. Her friend picked a name from a list of potential Military pen pals to get a little insight on how to move on and she ended up emailing me."

I take a bite of pancake, drowned in maple syrup, relishing how good real food tastes. First In-N-Out, now this?

Heaven.

"Go on," she urges me, a slight smile on her face.

"Well, she just kept writing me, and I kept writing her back...then we had that attack at the base and she freaked out, she was crying and I just...I couldn't take it, Mama. I never want her to cry."

I look down, feeling slightly ashamed at describing how I feel about my girl.

Mama clears her throat and gives me a sympathetic look, urging me to keep going.

"And then we Skyped and she is just...God, Mama she's so beautiful. It's unreal. Then she came and got me yesterday when I landed and I took her to my spot on the beach."

I watch as she processes this, she looks to me and I know she gets me. She always does, even if I didn't say it out loud she knows exactly how I feel about Elli.

"Well baby, sounds like you're falling for this girl. How long did you say this has been going on?"

I take a moment to think back because even though I feel like I have known my sweet girl for so long, I realize it's only been about three and a half months.

I look up and Mama is still staring at me.

"Uh, been almost four months I think."

She sets her coffee cup down and walks around the island toward me and leans her back against it.

"Raiden, jump."

"Wha-"

She holds up her hand when I try to speak.

"No baby, just let me finish."

She takes my hand in both of her small ones.

"When your daddy was overseas, doing Lord knows what... It was really hard for me. I was pregnant, I was alone and I missed him with every piece of my soul." She squeezes my hand gently. "But when he was here, home with me, with you, I felt so unbelievably complete and happy. We had a one in a million kind of love. And just watching you describe this woman, I know that you're destined for the same kind of love."

I stand there struggling to absorb this. She lost my dad when I was only a boy, and after that, she just took care of me. Never remarried, never dated, it was always just the two of us.

"Being the hard-headed boy you are I know you're going to try to fight it, thinking you'll get hurt if you give your heart over." She puts a hand on my cheek. "But baby, if you feel for even a second that this woman is the one for you, then you give everything you have."

I lean down and envelop this wise woman in my arms, letting her know I heard her loud and clear even if it scared me half to death.

I do the dishes for her while she goes outside to tend to her garden and take a minute to look out the window at her, surrounded by the plants she nurtures every day.

She's right. I already know Elli is different, she's loved and lost but more than anything, I want to protect her and her heart. I know she's worth it. I just have to be patient with her.

Until she's on the same page as me, I just have to show her I am here and I'm not going anywhere.

I shake my head, already feeling myself drift so far from the man I was only a few months ago.

What is it about that one person that can so totally change you?

Chapter 28

~Elli~

"He didn't kiss you..." Jen's mouth is slightly ajar and I'm pretty certain her eyebrows are clear in her hairline.

I shrug, loading up our wine glasses once more.

"Yeah, I don't know...maybe I'm not what he was expecting, so he didn't kiss me?" I wince, really hoping I'm just being dramatic.

"Girlfriend, he took you to the beach and just absorbed your presence like some sort of high-end perfume... Fairly certain he's into you."

I smile, remembering how just a few nights ago I was wrapped in Raid's arms and nothing, no sorrow or worry could reach me.

"Okay, you love struck teenager, can we get back to the matter at hand?"

I narrow my swoony eyes at Jen.

"Hey, don't you give me that look, missy! I just want to hear about the juicy texty details!"

My eyes turn skyward, knowing she'll beat the details out of me if she has to.

Ah, best friends.

"Well, we have just been really flirty, it's like we already know each other. I feel like such a teenager."

I turn a little red admitting it but I totally do. It's like rediscovering the best parts of life all over again, a complete do-over. It's a little surreal to think I'm actually acting like this. But I don't think I would want to stop it even if I could.

Jen grabs her wine glass and sips, observing me.

"I like this, I like who you are right now. You're becoming my best friend again," she says quietly nudging me with her foot.

I give her ankle a gentle squeeze. "Yeah, I missed you too, bestie."

Awhile after Jen passed out on the couch, I went out and stood on my back deck.

Dahlia sniffing around the yard somewhere, only illuminated by the moon and stars.

It smells warm, of eucalyptus and moonlight.

I let the aroma fill my senses, washing over me.

Even though he isn't here with me anymore, I always talked to Garrett when I needed to purge my soul, let the hurt out. I haven't needed him as much lately only because Raiden has given me the same comfort and understanding.

Even if this thing with Raiden, whatever it is or isn't, goes anywhere or doesn't, I know this is the time to move forward.

Literally taking a step toward the yard I look up at the stars, whispering to my husband.

"Hi baby, it's me."

Crickets sound throughout the yard, the only sound aside from Dahlia's quiet snuffling.

"I think I have to let you go now."

Tears threaten to spill from my tightly closed lids but I keep talking.

"I will always love you, and I will always remember you, no one could ever replace you, G. I'll take you everywhere I go, and hold you close to my heart forever."

Tears dripping down my face I bring my hand up, placing a simple kiss in my palm and sending it skyward, sending Garrett one last piece of me.

The catharsis of letting go of my first love, my husband and the person that brought me both such happiness and unbearable pain in my whole life, fills me.

The fog that my life became suddenly feels less stifling. The weight of Garrett's death that sat on my shoulders for years seems to dissipate. My chest expands, letting the night air fill me up and leave no trace of the hurt behind.

I can do this.

Now the only thing left for me to do is follow my dreams, follow my heart and get my life back on track.

I can finally start mending the relationships I so carelessly took advantage of when I was hurting. I no longer need to feel guilty for wanting, for yearning to become a woman again and not live this life as just a widow. I know in my heart that I will never love Garrett any less but I also know that there is more to living than just taking in a breath and calling it breathing. It's okay to take that proverbial step forward.

A cold nose to my hand tells me it's time to go back inside, my midnight speech over and done with.

I allow my dog to lead me inside, herding me being one of her favorite things to do. Up the stairs we go until we get to my bedroom door, opening it for her she goes to sniff around before plopping on the bed. Rather than stay at the foot where she normally sleeps, she curls up by the pillows, somehow sensing that I need the company tonight.

I slip my lounge pants off and grab some shorts to sleep in, crawling in beside my girl.

Her eyes close as I stroke her between the ears, already drifting off to sleep. If only it were that easy for me to fall asleep.

My thoughts turn to Raiden just as they so often do nowadays. I wonder what he's doing right now, probably asleep. Dahlia is nice to have here but I want to feel the strength of a man seep into my bones, not the silent support of my puppy dog.

I snatch my phone from the nightstand and tap a quick text to him, hoping like hell he's awake and thinking about me too.

Me: Hey you.

Not even a moment later I get a response, my chest getting tight, anticipation a heady drip into my veins.

Raid: Sweet girl, why are you up so late?

Sweet girl, his pet name for me does something utterly intoxicating to me. Just reminding myself of how it sounds spilling from his plump lips sends me off into a heady bliss.

Me: Can't sleep, I wish you were here…

I thought before I wanted to feel his strength, I more than want it. I crave it. Like a drug, I want him to shock my senses and keep me safe.
I want, and for so long I didn't think I could or would let myself want again.

Raid: I wish I were there too, baby.

Oh, can I please have more of that? Feeling brave, I ask the question burning me up.

Me: Why aren't you?

Did I really just ask that?
Okay, don't freak out Elli, he's just a guy – albeit a hot sexy piece of American soldier, all tatted up and tan

and oh, I have to stop thinking like that.

God, I need to get out more, or maybe just jump him or something.

My phone starts buzzing wildly in my hand with an incoming call from him.

I answer, my voice tickling my lips it comes out so breathy. "Raid, hi."

Then the sexiest sound in the universe comes across the line. "Baby," he says it on a low growl, his voice so deep and full of all the bourbon goodness I've come to love. It hits me like a lightning bolt right through my body. Right down deep into my core, drenching me.

The sheets surrounding me brush against my skin, my body so aware and ready like a live wire. From one single word, he did this to me.

"You really want me there?"

Just imagining Raid being here with me right now thrills and terrifies me. Thrills me for obvious reasons and terrifies me because I don't know how I'll keep my hands off him.

"Yeah, I really do."

I glance over at my alarm clock and see it's around one am, I hope he doesn't think this is a booty call, but maybe it could be?

"What's your address?"

Oh yes, yes I need to see him. I give him my address and then we hang up.

Cue me frantically rushing around making sure my room is tidy and my face doesn't look a disaster.

I hear my phone beep from somewhere on the bed and I know he's here. Oh God, I am so excited and nervous, what am I going to do now?

Raid: Outside, beautiful.

Me: Be right there

I leave a snoozing Dahlia on the bed to creep down the stairs and the hallway to the front door, moving on tiptoes as to not wake Jen. If the deep snoring coming from the couch is any indication, she won't be waking up anytime soon.

Excellent.

I crack open the front door, and there he is, leaning up against the door jam. He's in just a black T-shirt and shorts, his meaty biceps straining the material in the most delicious way.

I reach through the opening and grab his hand, a huge and probably wanton looking smile on my face and pull him through.

He doesn't say anything, just smirks down at me as I lead him up to my room.

I feel like a teenager again, sneaking a guy into my room. Not like I ever did that or anything, but this is exactly what this feels like.

I pull him into my room and close the door, moving my back against it.

Finally, I'm able to take in all the sexy glory that is Raiden Michaels.

I see Dahlia's head perk up, ready to get the intruder but I put my finger to my lips and she doesn't make a peep. Good doggy.

"Raid, this is my dog, Dahlia."

He walks over cautiously but with authority and she takes one sniff then nuzzles his hand.

Very good doggy.

He walks back over to me and in one swift move, pulls me into his arms, my own arms going around his waist and my head straight into his chest. He smells like body wash and all man. Not cologne but just him, a scent that is going straight to my head...and straight to my nether regions.

Calm down, girl.

We stand there for what feels like forever, but what also only feels like a second and then he releases me. It's one in the morning and Raid is in my room...in my house. I look up at him and he's smirking down at me.

"Elli," he says, and that's it.

I go up on my toes to wrap my arms around his neck and crash my lips against his. He hesitates in surprise at my bold move but only for a second and his arms are wrapping around my body so tight, his mouth moving against mine. His tongue parting my lips, seeking entrance.

And oh man, do I let him enter.

He's kissing me harder and harder and I feel like my whole body is on fire ready to explode in a ball of flame. Our kisses become more frantic as we get used to each other and want more, so much more. He lifts me up so I can wrap my legs around his waist, situating me right up against him in all the right spots.

Oh, yes. Yes, please.

I keep kissing him, his tongue knowing just how to stroke mine and make me come alive. We are kissing so hard I feel like I really will combust, so I start grinding up against him. Just as he starts to reciprocate I hear a low yip come from behind me.

I pull away and try to slow my breathing, feeling just how hot and swollen my lips are. I look sheepishly up at Raiden and all I see is unbridled passion staring back at me. If I were a glacier I would have melted to the ground with the heat radiating off of him. He's still holding me up, his hands gently cupping my ass. Have you ever been so consumed by lust you can't see straight? That's me right now. All I can do is try to wade through the haze and stare at how fucking handsome this man is.

His lips puffy from my own, those bright blue eyes staring at me, how his hands feel on my ass. I can't get over it. We haven't even said anything, just locked in this kind of limbo. Between what we just did and want we want to do. He's definitely into me. I blink, trying to get a handle on myself but really loving how wild I'm being.

"You're so handsome, Raiden." My voice coming out low and husky.

His soft lips tip up on one side in a smirk. I shift against him just slightly, reminding us both the position we are still in. The thing is, I don't want to break it. I want to be wrapped around him like a monkey. I don't want his hands to not be on my ass. Like an electric current is ebbing and flowing between us, like the tide coming in and out I feel so drawn to him. I have to give in.

Just as I'm about to lean in and take another kiss, Raiden growls. "Fuck it," he lunges toward me and attacks my lips.

This time there is no stopping it. His tongue snakes into my mouth, massaging my own and causing small whimpers to come out of me. We ramp up the speed and I am so beyond into it that I pull back so I can bite his bottom lip. Pulling it a little with my teeth, eliciting a growl from deep in his chest. The sound radiates down like a shot right to my clit. Our bodies are almost vibrating with need. Need for each other. Need for this to go further, to let go.

Dahlia needs to not be in here right now. X-rated make outs are not for puppies… I grip his strong biceps, feeling the ridges where the muscle is hard and defined and pull back, mourning the loss of his lips the second I do.

"Put me down for a sec." So he does.

I go to the door and snap for Dahlia to come so I can shoo her out the door. Once she's in the hall walking down the stairs to the living room where Jen is hopefully still passed out, I close the door and turn around, leaning my back against it.

Chapter 29

~Raiden~

She's leaning against her bedroom door. Her lips are swollen and pink. She's breathing heavy which is causing her full breasts to heave, drawing my attention perfectly. Her little short shorts are even shorter now because they've ridden up her thighs while her legs were around my waist. A feeling I crave to feel again. Her pussy perfectly lined up with my cock. A cock that is currently aching for some attention. Her eyes are saying something and I need to find out what it is.

I stalk toward her. Moving deliberately toward this tiny pixie, needing more of her. Her eyes never leave mine as I close the space between us and go to grab her. She surprised me when she kissed me first, but I am definitely not one to argue. I pull her to me and look down.

"Sweet girl, what are you doing to me?" My voice is harsh, my cock is raging and I need her. I just hope she needs me too.

She smiles, her eyes shining bright. "I think the proper question is, what are *you* going to do to me?"

Then she bites her bottom lip, taking it between her teeth.

I lose it. I lift her up again, her legs automatically going around my waist exactly where I want her. I move backward until I am right at the foot of the bed, and lay down. I want to fuck her. No doubt about that, I need to. But I want her to know she has control over this. The first time she needs to know it's her choice. Next time is another matter altogether.

I'm lying there and she sits up to straddle me, her tiny frame a perfect picture situated right on my cock. She sweeps her hair over her shoulder and leans down, pulling at my bottom lip with her teeth. Fuck, I like it when she does that. I put my big hands on her small waist, digging into her flesh only slightly but enough to make her whimper. She slips her tongue into my mouth again and she tastes like sugar. And I am a diabetic needing that sugar.

Just as I'm losing my mind getting lost in her mouth, thinking about how badly I need her she says it. She gives me the golden words.

"Raid...I want you."

If I wasn't gone before, I am now. I move my hand and grab her ass hard, moving her shorts up so it's just skin on skin. I have to feel her. Her soft skin, so hot in my hand. I run my fingertips along her hip and then I reach the line of her panties. They're lacy and would be so easy to move aside. I open my eyes to see hers closed, her lip is in between her teeth again and she's breathing hard. I brush my fingers forward, touching her pussy lips lightly, she shudders on top of me. My cock pulses, cheering me on. I use my other hand to wind through her hair and crush her lips to mine. I slip my fingers into the lace and feel how soaked she is. A growl erupts from my chest and she moans.

Her moan is like a sexual symphony to my ears. I slip a finger through her slick folds and I swear I die a little. Her pussy is soaked and my dick is so hard I'm sure I could pound nails with it. I move my middle finger inside and have no clue how my dick would actually fit because she is so tight it's like a vise on my finger. She moves away from my mouth to my ear and is breathing heavy, her breath hot on my neck.

"I want you to come for me, baby." I have to focus to use my voice, any and all brain function is all but nonexistent at this point.

I move my thumb to rub against her clit while my finger pumps slowly in and out of her. Her breathing picks up, coming out in short rapid puffs against my skin. Yes, get there, baby. I speed up my rhythm until she starts grinding against my hand, which is causing me to lose my damn mind. Fuck I want to be inside of her, making her come around my cock. I keep rubbing her swollen clit and I know she's close.

"R...Raaaaaaaiiiidddddd," she moans long and loud, and then her pussy gets excruciatingly tight and she shudders in a full body orgasm.

Music to my fucking ears. So beautiful. When her body stops trembling, she turns her head so she's looking at me, blue eyes still mostly glazed over in lust. I withdraw my hand from inside her body and make sure she's watching me when I slip my finger into my mouth, savoring how she tastes. Like cotton candy and sin rolled up into one. Her eyes grow wide and then she does the sexiest thing I have ever seen in my life. Licks her lips and gives me a little smirk. She likes me tasting her.

Fuck me.

I shift so she's lying next to me, my arms forming a little cage around her.

"How you doin' baby?"

She blinks, a modest pink blush dusting her cheeks. Her eyes are so bright it's like looking into the sun.

"I'm good, handsome, I'm really good." She looks down for a second then back up at me, and as for me I'm just, her, amazed at this woman. "Will you stay with me tonight?"

I don't answer, just pull her even closer to my body and kiss her forehead, feeling her relax into me. This, this is where I'm supposed to be. With my girl in my arms.

Chapter 30

~Elli~

Explosions. Fireworks. Niagra Falls. Everything colossal that comes to mind. That was me the second Raiden made me come. Actually, I think I almost passed out. The occasional date with my B.O.B. was all right. But this... this was on another level. In the capable hands of a man.

The past two years, thinking about having this kind of intimacy with someone who wasn't my husband was out of the question. When it actually came down to it, I think I was more than ready because not at any time did I have a second thought.

Now that I'm pulled close to Raiden's chest and I am in a state of unadulterated satiated bliss? No regrets. Not one. It's almost comical in a way. For so long I was afraid to do anything that might mean me moving on, but I did this. I basically jumped this super-hot guy... And I don't feel bad. It makes me smile.

I snuggle in closer, loving how it feels to be in Raiden's arms. His biceps flex against my skin and I love that too. He's so strong. I could feel it when he was handling me. It was absolutely delish.

And oh God when he sucked his fingers with me all over them... I couldn't even handle it.

I close my eyes, listening to his heart, beating so steady and strong. He's alive, here with me. It's been so long since I've heard a man's heartbeat. Thoughts of how weird that is float through my sleepy head as I fall asleep nestled into my Marine's chest.

I am beyond warm. My face is pressed into something warm and it definitely isn't my dog's fur.

Huh. What?

I peel my eyes open and am met face to face with an absurd amount of ink on a hard defined chest. The chest of a man. A man in my bed. A man I am currently pressed up against. I start to panic a little bit, then realize I am an idiot and it's just Raid.

Oh good.

I distance myself a bit and try to untangle our limbs.

"Mmm, was wondering when you were gonna wake up."

My eyes shoot up to his and they open slowly, giving me a panty-melting smile.

Oh Lord help me.

"How long have you been awake?" My voice is low, edged with sleep with a tint of lust.

Like I said, Lord help me.

"Couple hours, fell back asleep here and there."

I roll over so I can see what time it is on the alarm clock next to the bed and it's close to ten am.

"Raiden! You could've woken me up, I never sleep this late!"

He just shrugs. "I wanted to let you sleep, you seemed pretty comfortable."

I can't help but smile at how considerate he is. "Yeah, well I bet you were bored to tears."

"Actually," stretching his arms above his head, "I had some entertainment."

Two things cross my mind. One, when did he take his shirt off? Two, what!

I give him the side eye.

"And what entertained you?"

Sitting up, giving me the full view of his chest, abs, arms, oh my word.

"You were having quite the conversation in your sleep." He winks.

The big jerk just winks at me. As for me, I know my face is fifty shades of red and I am beyond embarrassed.

I shove his shoulder. "What! What did I say!"

He starts laughing, probably at my attempt to shove him, like it did anything.

"Oh, just about how hot you think I am." He winks again.

Oh he's gonna get it.

I fling myself at him ready to give him a piece of my mind but he anticipates it because he catches me and flips me so I'm pinned under him. I put on a grumpy face and stare up at him.

"You are so lying."

He kisses my nose. "Yeah, I am. But you didn't deny it did you?"

My lips quiver, trying to keep up the grumpy act and not bust into a wide smile.

"Is my girl gonna give me a smile?" I shake my head. "How about now?" he says, kissing my forehead.

"Nope."

He moves to my cheek and places a gentle kiss. "Now?"

"No way." On the inside, I am giddy as all hell but I like this game too much to stop now.

Moving to my other cheek he kisses it. "Not even now?"

I shake my head, totally about to fail at the not smiling thing. He gets close, his nose brushing against mine. My lips part as my breathing picks up. "Elli, you better smile for me." He narrows his eyes.

I shake my head no, our noses touching in an unintentional Eskimo kiss.

His voice comes out low and deep. "What about now?" His tongue snakes out and runs along the seam of my bottom lip.

Our breaths mingle together, our mouths so close. I'm so losing this game. I want to kiss him. I want to kiss him more than I want to breathe. My brain is shorting out, no other thoughts than just how badly

I need to taste his lips against mine. He must know this is how he's going to win this little game because he runs his tongue along my upper lip next. As if I am not already coming undone he moves one of his legs in between both of mine and applies just the right amount of pressure where I need it.

Oh Lord, I need it.

He's teasing my lips with his, brushing them lightly against mine, knowing exactly how he's driving me crazy. I let out a little whimper telling him he has to give me more. I don't know if I can take any more of this so I bring my hands up to try and crush him down on my lips but before I can get anywhere close he grabs both of my hands and shoves them above my head holding my wrists in one of his big hands. My eyes widen, never having been handled like that. It wasn't hurtful...it was hot.

He looks me in the eyes. "Nope, no touching." His voice is so deep and sexual. If an orgasm had a trigger noise, it would be Raiden Michael's voice.

He lowers his face down to mine once more and I'm ready to obey, I'll be a good little girl until he gives me what I want.

I'll try at least. No promises here.

He brushes his lips slowly and lightly across mine until I'm ready to whimper. Just as the noise creeps up my throat he presses his knee harder up against me, making my clit practically go nuclear.

Just as a screaming moan pierces through my throat, Raiden crashes his lips against mine, swallowing the sound whole. This kiss is different, this kiss is claiming. His tongue dominating mine, his lips so hard and soft at the same time, making me understand.

Understand who's in charge here.

His knee moves in circles against me and I am so close I can practically taste it. I moan again, the sound mingled with his deep guttural growl, his hand holding my wrists flexing and tightening. I grind up against him so close to release, wanting him so badly I can't even see straight. He takes his other hand and dives into my shorts and panties, the second he touches my swollen bud, I go cataclysmic. Behind my closed eyelids all I see are shooting stars and outer space.

I'm still moaning and Raid is slowing his kisses down, still swallowing my sexual noises, his hand stilling on my clit, so sensitive I shudder. He releases my hands. I open my eyes and he's staring down at me, an expression I don't recognize on his face.

"What is it Raid?" I whisper.

He presses his lips against mine in a tender passionate kiss.

"Nothing, baby girl, you're just so fucking gorgeous when you come."

Chapter 31

~Raiden~

She's so fucking beautiful. I don't even know how she's under me right now. I don't even know how we got here.

She's looking up at me with those baby blue eyes and I am so pussy whipped I can't even see straight. We're just locked in this moment, neither of us blinking, breathing, moving.

But of course, her friend decides right now is the time to interrupt. Three bangs on the door and it's open.

"Uhh…I see now that I should have waited until you answered me to come in…"

I look behind me at the doorway and there is Elli's best friend. Her mouth is fully open and it makes me chuckle. I roll off of my girl and she sits up, her hair looking wild and disheveled, her lips still noticeably puffy.

"Jennifer Irene. What the fuck!"

At that outburst, I fall back laughing.

Eli looks so pissed off and it's without a doubt the cutest thing I have ever witnessed. Jen just closes her mouth and backs out slowly, closing the door.

Face now in her hands. "Oh my goodness. I am so sorry, Raid." Elli's voice is a bit muffled but I still think it's funny.

I take her hands away from her face and kiss them.

"Let's go make some breakfast. I feel like it'll be less awkward if we at least go out there."

I get up and she just watches me. Almost as if she has a hard time looking away. I don't mind it, it gives my ego a huge boost knowing she likes what she's seeing. I grab my shirt and slip it over my head, then readjust the rock hard issue in my shorts.

Yes, that is twice I've gotten her off.

Yes, I am still excruciatingly hard.

And yes, I want to fuck her brains out...but that time will come.

When we finally get to the kitchen, I have myself under control. Jen is sitting at the counter with Dahlia by her feet and she's drinking coffee, a bottle of Advil already out on the counter next to her. She turns around when she hears us.

"So...what exactly did I just walk in on Elli?" She doesn't sound accusatory, but actually happy and curious.

I can see her eyebrows creeping up into her hairline and it's pretty funny honestly.

"I mean, I think the situation kind of explains itself, Jen." Elli is blushing so hard I can practically feel it radiating from her.

I love it, she's so fucking beautiful. I can't get over it. She walks over and grabs two cups from a tall cupboard, going up on her tiptoes, her shirt raising up to expose the soft supple skin at her waist. I can't help but just stand there like a dolt staring at her skin, knowing how it feels against my skin, like cream and sugar and everything sweet. I could eat her up. I need to taste her. The need to feel her body against mine again is borderline overwhelming.

She glances up at me and I swear she can read my thoughts. She pulls her lip in between her teeth while she's staring back at me and it takes every ounce of strength I have not to grab her and take her across the counter.

Jen needs to leave. Or I need a cold shower. Either way, something has to be done about this.

"Actually, I think I better head home and tend to a much-needed hangover rest day," Jen chirps, sliding off of her stool.

"You sure Jen? You're good to stay you know."

Elli and Jen catch each other's eyes briefly as if to ask if they're okay.

"Love you, girlfriend...Nice to meet you, Raiden."

She waves at me as she's backing out of the kitchen so I nod my head and reply, "You too, Jen."

As soon as the front door closes, I sigh a breath I hadn't realized I was holding. It truly is just Eli and I now.

"Raid," she says it so softly I almost don't hear her.

I turn around and she's so close, close enough to smell her. She smells like my mama's garden, wild and earthy, yet so feminine and fragrant.

"I just...I wanted to thank you for coming over last night and for staying with me." She hangs her head like she's ashamed.

I put a finger under her chin to force her to meet my gaze. "Baby, you don't have to thank me. I wouldn't wanna be anywhere else."

Her eyes are like light pools of water, so crisp and clear, I want to dive right in them. I slide my finger across her jaw just as she's closing her eyes I make my way to the back of her neck under her hair. Her eyes are now fully closed so I take my time and move in slow, my big hand cupping her slight neck. I run my nose down her cheek to her neck and then to trace her collarbone, just breathing her in and relishing the fact that this is all new. This is all happening now, I can explore her body the way I've been craving to.

She's barely breathing, anticipating what I'll do next. I slip my tongue out and take her right at the base of her neck where I can feel her pulse rapid fire under her soft skin. She sucks in a sharp breath. This slow game is eating me alive when all I want to do is eat her.

I move slowly up to her ear and whisper, "Tell me what you want, baby." I don't even notice her gripping my waist until her hands flex in my shirt. The most seductive whisper I've ever heard hits me like a freight train.

"You."

That's it, exactly what I wanted.

With no further hesitation, I pick her up so her legs go around my waist and carry her back to her bedroom and kick the door shut behind me. Last night was to show her I won't push her if she isn't ready. This was the green light and fuck, I am already outta the gate heading toward the first quarter mile turn.

I throw her onto the bed then rip my shirt over my head, sending it sailing across the room. Her breathing gets progressively shallow as she takes in all my ink over my defined and well-used muscles. I climb up the bed, so I'm on top of her thinking to myself the whole way that she is wearing entirely too many clothes.

As I'm moving north I take my hands and catch the hem of her T-shirt raising it up her toned stomach, kissing the swell of her tits and oh fuck, I'm in heaven just seeing those perfect rose colored nipples puckered and just waiting for my mouth to be on them.

Who am I to deny such a request?

I bend my head down, catching her eyes briefly, and suck a tight rose bud into my mouth, shit she tastes like whipped cream. I lightly bite and tease her with my teeth, just enough to get her to start grinding underneath me and panting. She goes to put her hands in my hair, but this is my time. I grab her wrists and put them above her head, a sexy gasp escaping her lips at my roughness. I move up to her neck and place a possessive claiming bite there at the base of her throat.

Mine.

She might not get it yet, but I can't leave her alone now, I've tasted her and I need to have her.

Keep her.

Make her mine.

She starts to writhe under me and I almost shoot my load right there in my shorts.

Nu uh baby, not yet.

I keep her hands above her head, locked there with just one of my big hands holding both of hers and use my other to softly skim over her skin down to her shorts. I tug them down working one side down then the other and when she's bare I can smell how wet she is for me, it ratchets up my desire for her tenfold.

I can't take it. I'm an animal and she's my prey.

My lips touch her collarbone gently, contrasting what I'm about to do next. I let the pads of my fingers trail up her thighs, my kisses becoming more urgent, turning to biting and sucking then I move my fingers through her drenched pussy lips and I lose myself in how slick she is. It's driving me wild. I press my thumb against her clit and I swear she almost comes undone right there.

She's panting and grinding against my hand so I withdraw it and look into her eyes.

I growl out, "No baby, that orgasm is mine and you can have it only when I give it to you."

Chapter 32

~Elli~

His words force my brain to short out and all I can focus on is how bad I want to feel him. I know he's big, he's been pressed up against me this whole time and the longer he goes teasing me, the more I want him. It even goes beyond wanting something. I have never known what it's like so completely *needing* to be filled. I want him to be rough, the way he is holding my hands pinned above my head is so hot I'm practically on fire. I'm breathing so hard like I've been sprinting for the past hour. One of his hands is holding both of my wrists captive above my head and it's difficult not to struggle against him. The more I struggle, the closer I get to claiming ecstasy. All I want is for him to fill me and to be honest, those thoughts thrill me, and scare me to death. I've never wanted anyone like I want Raid. I know if we take this to where we both want to, there won't be a way back. We won't be two strangers thrown together by email, by similarities that weave back and forth between us. We'll know everything. No going back.

Do I want this?

Am I ready?

When I look up and into his eyes, I know with every single cell in my body that I do. I want Raiden Michaels. He has a power over me that crashes into me with enough force to knock me silly. I never want to lose this.

He catches me staring and smirks, bending his head to softly graze his lips against mine. A contrast to how hard our bodies are against each other. When he pulls back, I can see the passion blazing in his eyes, mirroring my own.

"Raid, please," I whine. I can't help it. It's like I'm under a sex spell where the only thing I can think about is feeling him inside me.

He growls, a sound that shoots straight to my core and I practically come right there. I slam my eyes shut, the pleasure from just his noises almost breaking me apart. He lets go of my wrists but I leave them up there, loving how it felt when he held them. His weight is lifted off me so I open my eyes, already getting upset that I can't feel his body against mine. He leans back on his heels and tears off his shirt, my eyes moving to take in every inch of his tan tattooed skin.

I lick my lips, wanting to trail my tongue down each and every ridge of muscle. He watches me watching him and stands up. I know he's teasing me, dragging out this dance between us until I scream, and oh, I am so close to screaming. I've come so close, I crave release like a junkie. He hooks his thumbs in his shorts and then they're on the ground. I almost choke on my tongue and start coughing, my eyes as big as the moon.

"Raid...that isn't going to fit." I motion to his rock hard cock, jutting out in all its glory.

He chuckles, deep and low in his throat. "Baby, it'll fit. But getting it there is half the fun, isn't it?"

He slinks down to bed again, smoothing his hands up my hot flesh, making me moan and squirm.

"Stop moving or you won't be getting anything" he grinds out, his erection bobbing between us hitting my inner thigh.

"God, Raid you're killing me." I breathe out, wanting to close my eyes in frustration but knowing I shouldn't miss a second of his slow assault up my body.

He plants a kiss on my hipbone, tongue snaking out to leave a white-hot mark on my skin.

I moan, "Raiden!"

When he laughs against my body I can feel it in my sex and in my soul. What felt like years of him making his way up my body suddenly came to a halt and he was right there, giving me those blue eyes and making me come undone just with a look. He brings his hand up to my neck and traces a pattern with his thumb.

"Elli, I need you to be certain about this." He looks fearful, that this might ruin us when we haven't really begun.

I bring a hand down and smooth it across his cheek, his stubble sending sparks through my palm.

"This..." I start. "Us, you and me right here, right now...I'm not afraid... I'm not hurting anymore. I feel alive." I look right into his eyes and will him to understand me. "Raid, I want you more than anything. I've never wanted someone so much in my whole life."

His eyes get big as he takes my words in.

I just lay there, this big handsome caring man, on top of me and see realization and resolve come over him. I don't have to be a wounded woman anymore. I can be whomever I want. And I want to be his. My heart beats so hard I feel that people on the space station can hear it.

Before I have a chance to worry if my words were too much too soon for him, he growls and crashes his lips against mine. All the heat and all the passion rolling over us like a thunderstorm. He rolls us so I'm straddling him, finally able to rub my clit against him, my wetness ratcheting up the intensity tenfold. I am already so close to falling over the edge, so close, but he grabs my hips and stops me right before I take it. I let out a scream in frustration, which only proves to make him laugh.

"Raid." Now it's my turn to growl. "Why. Are you. Doing. This. To. Me," I grind out, two years of pent of sexual need lacing my words.

"I stopped you because I want to be inside you when I come baby, not when you're grinding against me."

My mouth pops open into a surprised O and I blush. I didn't realize he was nearly as affected as me. I'm still letting that sink in when he expertly delves a hand between us rubbing my clit and sending me off into oblivion.

"Oh God, Raid!" I cry out, my body pulsing, grinding as much as I can against his cock, panting, swearing, and needing more.

"Good girl, now it's my turn." Raid flips me over and dives for his shorts on the ground, coming back with a condom and tearing it open. I watch with hazy lust filled eyes as he rolls it down the length of his cock and my mouth is watering just looking at it. He comes back to me and positions himself at my entrance, searching my eyes out for permission.

The second his tip glides against my folds, I fist the sheets at my sides. "Yesssssss."

Without any more hesitation, he presses into me, and I thought I was prepared but he is so big. I feel him stretching my tight walls as he goes deeper, my grip getting tighter, breaths becoming shorter. I can hear him groaning but all I can focus on is how incredibly and deliciously full I am.

"Oh my God, Raid." I can't believe I even spoke, the moans spilling from my lips making it impossible to form thoughts or words.

He slides in to the hilt and I nearly scream, his lips coming down to pepper hot kisses up my neck to my ear where he bites me.

"Yes baby, say my name," he whispers.

I moan, I can't help it. Hearing him makes me want to explode into a ball of flames. He pulls out, moving back in slowly, the ache fading and the slow build of another orgasm beckons. He starts moving faster, taking my hands in his and raising them over my head again. Pinning me down with his thrusts and killing me with pleasure. He uses his other hand to grasp my hip, starting to pick up his pace until he's slamming into me. Our sweaty bodies slap against one another, tangled in ecstasy.

"Oh Raid, I'm so close," I get out in between moans, getting louder and louder with each thrust.

"Come for me, Elli, come for me and only me," he says in my ear. "Come now, baby, coat my cock."

Like a trigger point, I detonate, screaming his name and writhing beneath him while he pumps into me with even more force and passion. He yells out when I feel my pussy constrict around his big cock and he growls deeply when he comes, thrusting into me three more times, letting me milk every last drop.

Chapter 33

~Raiden~

I'm still inside her and I don't think I have ever seen her look more radiant. Her skin is slick with sweat and her hair is a tangled mess but she looks so unbelievably relaxed that it knocks the breath from my lungs.

She lays there, still pulsing around my cock, making me want to take her all over again and has such a look of being totally sated and happy that I can barely stand it when I pull out.

I leave her to flush the condom and bring a warm washcloth I snagged from her bathroom to clean her up. I make my way to her and she turns her head to watch me, then a better idea comes to me. I toss the washcloth when I reach the bed and her eyes question what I'm about to do.

I scoop her up in my arms and carry her into her bathroom, pausing to flick on the shower, and then set her down on the counter. I wedge myself between her legs, my dick already wanting more and standing at attention, rubbing ever so softly against her pussy.

Quicksand

She makes a low humming noise in the back of her throat, her eyes closing and letting herself feel. I shove my hands in her hair and tilt her head up so I can see her eyes. She opens them and looks right at me. Not a single shred of fear in her eyes.

Not one doubt.

Not one worry.

Just her and I in this moment, no ghosts haunting us. This woman does something to me, the way her eyes are making me want to sit at her feet and worship her. The way her body fits perfectly against mine, the way I felt inside of her, stretching her and filling her up until I thought we both might pass out. I look down at her and feel things I never thought I would feel. Things that seemed crazy and outlandish to me only months ago.

I press my lips against her forehead and she leans into me, her small hands landing on my hips. I take a deep breath, inhaling her scent and then I pick her up and she wraps her legs around my waist so I can take us into the shower. I set her down on her feet but only so I can lather every inch of her sacred body in soap, even washing her hair and massaging her muscles.

She moans and wiggles beneath my hands but I just keep going. Not even bothering with myself. I rinse us both off and step out, grabbing two fluffy towels from the cabinet next to the shower. I towel dry her then spend extra time getting the water out of her hair, all the while knowing she's watching my every move. I wrap one towel around my waist and hang up the other, wanting her naked.

I pick her up again, just to carry her over to the bed. Her hair fans out over the pillow when I lay her down and all I can think is how beautiful she is, and unlike any woman I have ever had.

"Elli, can I get something off my chest?"

Her eyes flash with uncertainty and fear but then it's replaced with compassion. "Of course, honey, anything."

I lay down next to her, draping my arm over her stomach and pulling her back to me. I bury my face in her neck and breathe her in again.

"Sweet girl," I start, "I never really have relationships." I can hear her swallow. "What I mean is that I never stick around long enough, never had anyone who I wanted to wait for me through tours." She swallows again and I hear her breathing change. "Don't freak out, I just..." I stop, unsure of how to continue.

"You just what, Raid?"

I sigh, how do I even say this?

"I just haven't done this before, baby, this is all new to me. I'm navigating something I have never done before."

She turns so she can face me, placing a gentle hand on my cheek. "You honestly think I know what I'm doing, Raid?"

I let out the breath I was holding.

"This is all new to me too, I was obviously married before but this just isn't the same as Garrett. This is all brand new and it's scary."

My eyes flash with hurt and fear. I don't want her to be scared, what if she gets scared and can't do this? What if the pain is too much for her?

"But," she kisses my lips ever so softly, soothing away the fear, "scary is good, scary means I'm feeling, that I'm alive. You make me feel alive."

I don't hold myself back any longer and kiss her with everything I have. Every doubt and insecurity for us, every bit of anger I have toward Garrett for leaving her and every ounce of thankfulness I feel for him leading her to me.

Chapter 34

~Elli~

"Jen, seriously I almost cried."

She's already drained her glass and is pouring a second, I, on the other hand, don't need wine to be drunk. I am still very drunk off Raiden.

We're sitting in her living room and the sun is setting, bathing the walls in oranges and pinks. It's only been about twenty-four hours and Raid and I haven't stopped texting once. He left after we ate greasy pizza in bed, naked, I might add. Then he kissed me stupid and promised to come see me when he was done with work.

Work, that scares me.

I don't want anything to happen to him that would affect him like it did Garrett. But he assured me that as long as he is on American soil I have nothing to worry about and I have to believe him. Plus, I know he misses Weston when he doesn't see him. I can just tell from all the stories he brought up when we were together in bed, learning about one another.

Quicksand

"So it was really that big, like you're not just exaggerating?" Jen has her eyebrows raised and I can tell she doesn't believe Raiden was the biggest ever, and honestly the most intense intimate sex I had ever had. Which makes my heart ache a little, something I will just have to get used to, knowing this is so much different than my marriage.

"Jennifer, I am not lying. Look at me! I can barely sit down comfortably!" I gesture to my lady business and she busts out laughing. I throw a pillow at her but she dodges it and sips from her glass.

"Elli, you are too much. I truly thought you were going to punch me when I walked in on you two!" She starts laughing again and I join in because she's totally right, I almost did.

"Yeah well, you're lucky you're my best friend."

She looks at me pointedly then melts into a smile, "Yeah I am lucky."

I look down at my hands, clutching the wine glass. It probably wasn't easy for Jen to sit back and watch me wallow after Garrett died. I think that I was just so busy living in my own hell that I forgot I had people there to support and love me. Maybe if I would have listened to her sooner I could have started moving on and forgiving him...

"Babe, I am really, really from the depths of my soul, sorry I pushed you away when I was hurting." I look up at her and feel the tears threatening from the corners of my vision. "I...I honestly think I was at the point where I didn't want to go on any longer when you forced me into messaging a soldier. I don't know if you realize this, but I think you saved me." I let the tears fall and I can tell she's about to cry too and she leans over pulling me into a hug, careful not to spill the wine.

"E, you are more than my bestie, you are without a doubt, the closest thing to a sister I will ever have. I love you so much, girl." I hug her tight and laugh at how weepy we both are. "I have to get real with you here though."

I lean back and look at her, "Yeah?"

She nods and takes a sip of wine. "I pushed you into messaging someone to try and get you to move on, but I could have never imagined that would result in you falling tits over ass."

She sips again and eyes me. I know my eyes are huge and I let out a huge snort.

"Jen, this isn't...I don't think that..." I just sit there letting her words sink in.

Do I love Raiden?

Am I ready to love someone again?

Is there enough love even left after Garrett?

Jen must be reading my thoughts because she says very quietly, "I know you're going to fight this sweetie, you are going to resist until you're blue in the face." I look up at her and urge her with my eyes to keep going. "That's okay, for right now. But he's going to realize he feels the same way and you're going to need to be open to what comes after. Don't close your heart up Elli, you have so much love and light in you to give, don't forget that." She drops that word bomb on me and just gets up and casually walks into the kitchen. Giving me space enough to digest everything, she really is my best friend.

Chapter 36

~Raiden~

It's been a week and I've been so busy I haven't been able to go see my sweet girl. It kills me just having had her and now being so far away. I guess I'm being dramatic because until about a month ago I was oceans away from her but now that I've been inside her... something in me has changed. I can't stop thinking about her, I can't stop wanting to touch her skin, taste her, feel her. It's such a sweet addiction. I'm lost thinking about Elli when Weston snaps his fingers in my face, breaking me from my haze.

"Earth to Raiden, hello?"

I shake my head and swat at his hand still hanging there in front of me.

"Sorry man, just got distracted."

He motions with his head to a trail that runs the perimeter of the base and I nod. Running would probably do me some good. I haven't been able to gain any traction with my superiors on getting out of the Corp and it's eating at me. Weston seems to know exactly what I need to get all my frustration out. We run for a mile and a half before Weston spoke.

"Raiden, brother can I talk to you about something?"

I slow down to a walk and he does too.

"Yeah man, anything." I give him my full attention.

"Remember on tour when I was having those nightmares?" I nod, wiping the sweat from my forehead. "I keep having them."

I stop and turn to face him. Now that I am actually paying attention and really looking at my best friend, I can see he has dark circles under his eyes. His stubble is longer than he normally keeps it and he just looks worn out.

"What are they about, man?" I had all but forgot about his nightmares until now, I had been so wrapped up in my own world I forgot just how worried I was about him when we were in the desert.

He looks at me and sighs, "Death, I just see all the death."

I shake my head, wishing that there was something I could do for him, but at the same time knowing that there isn't.

"Wow, Weston. Have you looked into maybe seeing someone?"

He shakes his head, anger flashing in his features before it's soothed and he goes back to just looking tired. "Nah man, I'll be okay. Just wanted to get it off my chest."

I put my hand out to touch his shoulder, "You sure?"

He smiles and me and shakes my hand off. "Yeah, really I feel better already."

He takes off into a quick paced run and effectively ends the conversation. I run to catch up to him but he stays ahead of me until we're back to our trucks. He hops in and gives me a wave. He says he's okay but...I just wish I believed him.

Chapter 36

~Elli~

I smooth down my dress again and gaze at my reflection in the mirror. This woman staring back at me is someone I haven't seen in such a long time. I bring my eyes up from scanning my features and really search my face. I don't see the dark circles anymore that used to accompany my daily appearance. I don't see the lingering sadness that used to surround me and go with me everywhere.

I see someone ready to live. I see someone who I thought I would never be again.

Before I got married I was a shy but tenacious girl. I lived with my parents in a small town and we were like the three musketeers. My mom got sick when I started high school and I didn't handle it very well. That's when Garrett came in and showed me kindness and love. He was the football star of the school and I was the mousy little blonde who didn't really want to make the effort to be included in any of the cliques. He had to really go out of his way to be around me. I thought he was so handsome but I really didn't fall for him right away.

It was a slow build that resulted in a beautiful marriage...until the end. He was truly my best friend and my confidant, he did everything for me. I think what I miss most about him was having someone to talk to all the time, someone who knew me so completely that he could practically read my thoughts without me having to give any indication.

I shake my head, my ponytail swinging behind me. Raid's already given me that back and I've known him a fraction of the time I knew my husband.

Is this how it's supposed to happen?
Is this what I read about in my books?

I smirk, the anticipation of seeing my guy again and actually going out on a date. Gosh, I haven't been out on a date in what feels like forever. I smile, loving how my face actually lights up again.

I check my phone and it reads six o'clock, only fifteen minutes and Raiden will be here. I take one final look at my reflection and turn to head down the stairs to wait. Dahlia walks in front of me headed straight for the back door so I open it for her and follow her out to sit on the bench and watch her sniff around the yard. I look out at my yard and my dog and just don't feel the gaping emptiness that used to saturate my life. I'm sitting there absorbing feeling so uninhibited, completely unaware of my surroundings when I hear the back door open, which then causes me to jump three feet in the air, clutching my chest.

I spin around and there is Raiden with the most terrified look on his face, which only causes me to start laughing so hard I start wheezing.

"Oh my...fuck babe, I'm sorry for scaring you!"

I bend over and clutch my chest still laughing. He drops the flowers I just noticed he had and rushes over to me. He bends down and puts his big hands on my face, forcing me to look at him.

"Raid, really I'm okay." I straighten up and lean my cheek further into one of his hands. "Hi, handsome."

He smiles down at me and I swear my heart tries to beat out of my chest to get closer to him.

"Hi, sweet girl."

Oh, there goes my heart again.

He stares down at me with an emotion I can't quite place but I consider it to be a good one because he leans down and plants a soft kiss on my lips. When his lips brush against mine it's as if someone poured gasoline on me and lit me up with a match.

I let out a moan and wind my hands up to the back of his neck to pull on the hair there. He lets out a growl and kisses me harder, putting his hands on my waist and gripping me to him. I lean back and pant, really wishing that there were more of the hot kisses and less of the obstructive clothes. As if he can read my very naughty thoughts, he leans his forehead against mine and lets out a deep sigh.

"Baby if you keep that up, we won't be going on our date."

I swear his eyes turn into smoldering embers when I put on a sheepish smirk and bite my lower lip.

"I'm okay with that."

I really feel that Raiden growling is my new favorite sound in the world because every time he does it, I go zero to one hundred in the drenched panty department. I love how my body picks up on every vibe he's giving off. I've never been so totally in tune with someone else. He finishes growling at me and soaking my panties in the process, then grabs one of my hands and spins me around in a circle.

He lets out a low whistle. "Baby you sure are beautiful." He says it with such a strong inflection of devotion that it almost causes my knees to give out.

I can't even speak he has such an effect on me. He spins me into him and then we're dancing. Moving back and forth, to no music at all just the sound of our breathing and our heartbeats. He moves us so effortlessly, me so small in his big muscular arms. We fit together so perfectly. We keep moving like this, dancing in slow circles together when I feel a cold nose in the back of my knee. I giggle, Dahlia's nose tickling my skin. Raid stops us and bends down to pet her behind her ears which causes her to drop to the ground and demand belly scratches which he then happily provides. I can't help but laugh seeing this big guy wrapped around one spoiled dog's little paw.

"Okay Dahlia," he says straightening back up to tower over me. "Stay here, watch the house, good dog." She perks up at "good dog" and follows us inside.

Raid takes my keys and makes sure to secure the house before opening his truck's passenger side door and helping me up, copping a feel of my booty in the process. I feel so light and happy that it just makes me giggle some more. I love feeling so free and peaceful, finally.

He starts up his truck and heads out to the highway.

"Am I allowed to know where we're going?" He glances over at me and smiles.

It strikes me then how much I love making him smile. I don't know if I am the sole reason for it or what but when that man smiles…I feel like falling in love with him.

"Well, we are stopping at my house then I have a surprise for you."

I angle my body so I can face him more fully and reach my hand out, stroking his bicep. He immediately shivers and I love that I can affect him like he does me. I stay facing him, the side of my head leaning against the headrest until we reach his house.

He gets out and I watch him round the front of his truck until he's standing right there, waiting for me. He offers me a hand and I take it, feeling the sparks fly up my arm making my whole body tingle with excitement.

We barely make it to the front door before it flies open and standing before us is a woman only slightly taller than me with rich brunette hair and at least half of Raiden's gorgeous features. They have the same eyes and I immediately love her for it. Before either of us can introduce me, she steps off the porch and rushes at me, arms wide open.

"Oh honey, I am so happy to meet you!" She pulls me in and hugs me with enough force to make me believe she wrestles bears in her down time.

I laugh and hug her back as hard as I can. "I am so glad to meet you, Mrs. Michaels."

She steps back, her hands still gripping my shoulders. "Call me Rita, honey."

Raid chuckles from somewhere near us. "Mama you could have at least let her get in the door before you mauled her."

She tuts at him, which looks hilarious because of their size differences and pulls me in the door, Raiden following not far behind.

Chapter 37

~Raiden~

Honestly, I worried Mama wouldn't like Elli. Every time I thought about bringing her over I would start feeling angsty and panicky. I never brought home a woman before, not when I was in high school and definitely not between tours. There wasn't any point, those girls never stuck around to mean something, I made sure of that.

I already know Elli is different, I feel differently around her. Like I am a changed man, I don't even know how I was satisfied with what I had before. I could never just drop her, I think I'm too far gone now especially.

I realize now that I should have brought her over sooner, any doubts I had, disappear as I watch Mama lead her into the kitchen and sit her on a bar stool, chattering away about things I don't care to listen to. I'm too busy taking in the scene before me, my two favorite women in the world in the same room getting along really very well. It makes my heart do funny things in my chest, reminding me just how much Eli affects me. I stay silent, love being around both of them and their infectious energy.

After this, I plan on taking my girl back to my favorite spot on the beach and giving her a night she'll never forget. I received some good news from my superiors today and I can't wait to tell her. I haven't even told Mama yet but I know she'll love that I won't be in dangerous situations any longer. I don't even really know what I am going to do when I get out but I feel at this point I could do anything I wanted.

Mama is still chewing Elli's ear off and she is absolutely soaking it up. I love how well they're getting along. I feel my phone start vibrating in my pocket so I pull it out and see it's a text from Weston.

Weston: Can't do it anymore, man.

Me: What do ya mean? Do what?

Weston: Too many lives lost, they fucking haunt me.

I stare down at my phone, the only sound I hear is the blood rushing through my ears. This just doesn't feel right, something is so terribly wrong.

Me: Where are you?

Quicksand

Weston: Doesn't matter. This ends now.

I can't see, I can't breathe. My best friend. Fuck, not my best friend.

I don't register Elli coming up to me, I don't hear Mama gently calling my name. I am so numb and so terrified that my best friend is going to kill himself and that I'll be too late.

Too late. Fuck I have to go.

I shake my head and my girls are standing in front of me fear written on their faces. "I...I... It's Weston." Elli's face goes deathly pale and she turns to Mama.

"Rita, we have to go." She frowns but doesn't say anything else, just puts a loving hand on my shoulder before we walk out the door.

I hop in the truck, forgetting to be a gentleman and open my girl's door for her but she climbs up without a fuss and tells me to drive. I don't know what I would do if she wasn't here telling me what to do. I have so much unimaginable fear in my heart that I can barely operate.

"Raid," she says so softly I almost don't hear her. I look over, my face stoic. "You need to pull out of it." She doesn't continue, she doesn't offer any words of strength or advice, just "you need to pull out of it."

She's right.

I am a United States Marine, I can fucking handle this.

I punch the accelerator headed toward Weston's house. Thankfully he isn't far and it takes us no time at all. I just pray we aren't too late. I pray he's actually there.

"Elli, I need you to stay here." She opens her mouth to argue but I give her a warning look.

If something already happened I don't want her anywhere near it. I hop out and slam the door to my truck, taking off to the front door.

I open it when I realize it isn't locked. It's so dark in here, the sun having gone down only thirty minutes ago but there aren't any lights on inside. I feel along the wall for a light switch and flip it on when my fingers brush up against it. My eyes take a second to adjust to the sudden brightness and when they do all I want is to slam them shut. Weston is sitting on the floor, back against the wall that leads to his living room, with a 9mm in his hand. I can see the safety is off and he doesn't so much as glance my way when he notices I'm here.

"Weston, buddy you need to look at me," I say it softly but with authority, hoping his military training will trigger a response to command.

He turns his head slowly toward me and when I take in his features, I feel my heart crash through my body and land at my feet. His eyes are bloodshot and full of sorrow, blue almost black circles are shadowed under them and he looks about ten shades more pale than normal.

I drop to my knees to get on his level and start to move toward him. He watches me and tightens his grip on the gun. I notice it and stop moving, not wanting to cause him to make any rash decisions.

"Weston, I need you to talk to me."

He moves his eyes in my direction but he looks right through me. He pauses for a few beats then speaks quietly and full of anguish.

"I just can't live with this...this fucking guilt."

He throws his head forward between his knees, then back as hard as he can into the wall behind him. It startles me but still I move to get closer to him, feeling the time slipping through my fingers like sand.

"Buddy, it's going to be okay. We can get you someone to talk to."

He levels his gaze at me and the hair on the back of my neck stands on end.

"I survived when they died. Our brothers. Died. Raiden, DON'T YOU GET THAT?" His tone rattles me, this person in front of me isn't who I know, I don't know this man. He shakes his head in disgust at me and brings the gun up to his face, examining it with sick curiosity.

"Weston, I'm begging you, man, put it down."

He smirks, chilling my blood. He throws his head back in a cold laugh so I use that to my advantage, moving to tackle him to the floor. He may be down right now but he's just as strong as I am and he's desperate. He throws an expert punch and it strikes me in the temple, rendering me dizzy, giving him enough time to get on top of me. I reach up to knock him over and we're locked in a deadly wrestling match. The gun is clutched by both of us, one hand over the other, waving in the air pointing right toward the open doorway. I almost have him off of me, the gun almost in my control. I am so close to having him pinned when he pulls the trigger. The gunshot nearly shatters my eardrums, ringing becoming the only sound in my world.

Somehow, amongst the aftershock of the bullet firing, a small feminine gasp floats in through the open doorway and nearly puts an end to my entire world.

Chapter 38

~Elli~

Can this really be happening right now? My stomach aches from being in knots so tight I think I might die with worry. Raid is in there with Weston who is clearly not in the right state of mind.

God what if he's already...no I can't think like that. He isn't Garrett. It isn't too late.

I let out a frustrated breath and slam my head back into the headrest. What am I doing? My guy is in there. Mine, my person is in there with someone who is going through what my husband went through. I have to do something. How am I still just sitting here!? I have to do something, anything. Maybe I can help.

I unbuckle my belt and start toward the house. The warm wind whips at my hair, the smell of eucalyptus tickling my nose. The front door is open and I hear Raid's voice speaking lowly to Weston.

"Buddy, it's going to be okay. We can get you someone to talk to." I pause, letting Raid talk to him.

You're doing good, give Weston options, sweetie, you can talk him down from this. I keep listening hoping that Weston is in a place where he will listen to his best friend and not do anything rash.

The wind picks up again so I don't hear anything until Weston yells, "Our brothers. Died. Raiden, DON'T YOU GET THAT?"

I flinch, he doesn't sound like he's going to listen. I have to get in there, I have to try to help. I can't let someone else go through the despair Garrett did. It wouldn't be right to let someone else fall victim to PTSD, to let them suffer.

I turn and stride again toward the front door with purpose. When I step up and into the entryway what I see has me clutching my chest and my heart absolutely breaking. Raid and Weston are rolling around on the floor, trying their very best to get the other on their back and or away from him. They are both so strong, they are both so willful.

I'm so stunned that I don't move when I see Weston get the best of my sweet Raid. I am so scared that I don't move when I know the gun that has been so tightly clutched by both men is pointed directly at me. The only thought that crosses my mind in that very moment is how much I love Raiden and how I hope with all my heart I live to let him know that.

Blinding pain.
Darkness.
Warmth.

Light.

No more pain.

Just warm light.

Warm hands.

"Open your eyes, Elli girl." Garrett?

"Come on love, open your eyes." Garrett.

When I open my eyes he's standing there in front of me. I attempt to look up at him but the light is too bright.

"Garrett, how are you here?"

He laughs, a laugh I loved more than life itself at one time. A time that seems so very distant.

"You came here to me my Elli girl, but you aren't meant to stay here."

I tilt my head, not understanding the meaning behind that.

"What? Where are we?"

He bends down so I can see his eyes.

"Heaven baby, we're in Heaven."

I shake my head, taking a step back, he steps with me.

"No, what about…what about Raiden?" I catch his eyes and they shine with such love and devotion it's nearly suffocating.

"He's waiting for you." He doesn't say it with any sadness, with any hatred, only acceptance, and happiness.

"Where, where is he?"

He takes his strong hands, hands I knew so well and held so many times and turns me around where the light isn't so strong, isn't so blinding.

"He's there, baby, waiting just for you."

I lean my head against his hand still resting on my shoulder.

"This is okay?"

He gives me a gentle squeeze and laughs again.

"He is everything I could have ever wanted for you Elli girl, he's brought you back to life when I all but killed you." He shoves me toward the dim glow and suddenly all the pain comes screaming back.

Chapter 39

~Raiden~

There were moments in my life that I had truly thought defined me and the man I would become. The day my dad died was one of them. Realizing that it would be Mama and I from then on out and that someday I would try to follow in his footsteps.

My first tour, where I learned what real brotherhood was and when I met the man that quickly became my best friend.

The first email from Elli. I didn't even realize that my whole world was about to be uprooted and completely flipped upside down.

The day I came home and saw one beautiful woman standing there waiting on my sorry ass, for reasons I will probably never fully understand.

I stare down at her small delicate hand in mine and know that every change she's the cause of has been a change I desperately needed. I let my eyes roam to the back of her hand where the IV lead is, wishing that I could take away the sting it'll cause when she realizes it's there. Up her tan buff arm that's swamped by the oversized gown the hospital put her in. Up her sweet neck where I know she smells like lilies. Her gorgeous eyes that I know hold so much truth, so much conviction, and so much strength. I turn her hand over and gently drop a kiss in her palm. Wishing more than anything that I could kiss her eyes open, kiss the gunshot wound on her stomach and kiss her soft lips every day for the rest of our lives.

"Sweet girl," I whisper. "What are you doing to me?" I kiss her palm again, letting my lips brush against her soft skin over and over. "We're barely getting started, you can't leave me here alone now." My heart aches. "Beautiful Eli," my voice cracks, the emotion crashing over me like a tidal wave. "I don't wanna figure this out on my own." The first tear falls and lands in her palm, gravitating toward the center. "Let me protect you." Another tear falls. "Let me be the man you turn to when it gets too hard." Another. "Baby, you need to wake up so I can catch all the stars in the night sky and hang them in your bedroom so you only see beauty before you close your eyes every night." I hang my head, resting it against her now soaking wet palm. "Sweet girl, I love you more than anything in this world and I need you to wake up so I can show you, so I can marry you." I let my tears fall, not ashamed in the least to cry over this incredible woman.

Quicksand

It's close to midnight and the hospital is running on a skeleton crew, making the whole place lose its hum and bustle that daylight brings. The machines assisting my girl are quietly beeping, reminding me of the situation she's in. My forehead is resting on her thigh, her hand held ever so preciously in my own. I'll never leave her, no matter what, no force on earth could make me. I close my eyes, feeling her warmth and wishing she would just wake up.

"Raid?" It's so very soft and quiet I don't believe I've heard it. She clears her throat and tries again. "Raid."

Music to my fucking ears. My eyes shoot up and I raise my head to see my girl staring right at me. The second I have her eyes she cracks a smile that forever will be seared into my memory as the smile that stole every single piece of my heart and soul.

"Baby," I whisper, barely keeping it together now. She lifts the hand that I had in mine and brings it to cradle my cheek.

"Raid I had a dream." I move my hand to cover hers, leaning my face further into her palm.

"Tell me about it." She shifts to sit up more and winces when she realizes she's injured. She shakes her head and gets comfortable again ignoring the wound completely.

"I was in Heaven and Garrett was there." I nod, urging her to continue. "He told me you were waiting for me and that I had to go back to you." Suddenly I can't even pretend to speak, so awash with emotion it's suffocating. "He said you brought me back to life."

I close my eyes and attempt to get ahold of myself, my eyes tight with unshed tears. "I was waiting for you, I waited for you to open those beautiful eyes, baby."

She smiles down at me tenderly. I move my face to kiss her palm, a place I've kissed so many times in the past twenty-four hours.

"Elli," I start but she interrupts me.

"Raiden Edward Michaels, I love you." I'm speechless. "I love you more than I could have ever thought possible, and I know you don't feel that way for me and we just were getting to know each other and…"

I stand up and move over her, my hands to either side of her face. She just looks up at me mid-sentence and freezes when she sees the look in my eyes.

"Elli Avery Hendricks, I love you with every fucking fiber of my being." Her mouth pops open in surprise and I take the chance to plant a kiss on her for the first time in what feels like a millennia. "I" kiss "Love" kiss "You" kiss. I lean back and smile when I see her blushing furiously.

"I love you too, Raid."

Music to my fucking ears.

Chapter 40

~Elli~

When Weston pulled the trigger he hit me right on the side of the stomach. He didn't hit any major organs or so I'm told (it feels like he did) but I lost a significant amount of blood. That would explain me having my little meeting with Garrett in Heaven, and I know with everything in me that I really was there with him. But he pushed me back because he knew it wasn't my time and that I had a man waiting for me that would do anything to protect me. I didn't even think about what happened after I was shot, but Raid told me that he knocked Weston out cold, took me to the hospital and stayed with me every moment.

The hospital gave me a transfusion, sewed me up and told me I had to stay for three days. It's finally the third day and good Lord am I ready to get back to my own place with my doggy and with my guy. Jen stopped by as soon as Raid would let her and said she had Dahlia at her place, and that she would literally kill me if I ever died. Makes sense right? What are best friends for?

I sit up in the bed, ready to be in one that doesn't have rails on the side, and where I can have my big hulking boyfriend in it with me when there's a knock on the door. Weston steps in and Raid stands up nearly knocking over the chair he was sitting in. Weston holds up a hand, just as I grab one of Raid's to keep him calm.

"I know, Raiden, I deserve that."

Raid growls but doesn't make any other indication that he's going to talk.

"Elli, I don't think there are even words to describe how incredibly sorry I am." He hangs his head and I can tell that he really means it. "I messed up really bad, I'm messed up really bad and it wouldn't be right for me to ask for your forgiveness…"

I clear my throat and sit up taller. "Weston, I won't pretend to understand the kind of mindset you were in when we came over." He doesn't say anything but pleads with his eyes for me to keep going. "PTSD is no joke, I lost my husband to it and I thank the Lord that we didn't lose you to it too." Raid tightens his grip on my hand letting me know he's there for me.

Weston steps forward and this time Raid doesn't try to stop him He comes to the other side of the bed and drops to his knees.

"Elli, I will never forgive myself." I hold my free hand out to him and he takes it.

"Weston I just want to make sure we help you any way we can."

He smiles at me, Raid smiles at me and my heart feels so full I can barely stand it.

Epilogue

~Raiden~

She's standing there looking out over the yard in a peach colored sundress with her hair down in loose curls, cascading down her back. Dahlia is sniffing around while Weston tends to the steaks on the grill and Jen is sitting on the bench sipping from her wine glass. I walk up behind Elli and move her hair to one side so that I can bend down and bury my face in her neck. She shivers and brings a hand up to run through my hair. We're celebrating me becoming a civilian and being accepted into the police academy. There's one final surprise I have up my sleeve, she just doesn't know it yet. I kiss her neck, breathing in her sweet lily smell.

"Sweet girl." She shivers again and tugs on my hair lightly, letting me know just how I affect her. I wrap an arm around her waist and pull her back into me, her soft giggling literally giving me life.

"This is perfect, Raid, I'm so full, so happy."

I kiss her neck again. "Good baby, I want you to be happy." I spin her around and start to sway her back and forth, dancing with her to a song no one else can hear. Right here, in my arms, I hold my entire world. She leans her head against my chest while I fish the ring out of my back pocket. It was my mama's and when I asked her for it, I thought she would never stop crying.

"Elli, I love you more than life itself. Every second I'm with you I feel inexplicably whole."

She breathes in deeply as I reach down to capture her left hand.

"Marry me and be my sweet girl for the rest of our days."

Her eyes fill with tears as she nods frantically yes.

She said yes.

Once the ring is resting perfectly on her left ring finger, she jumps into my arms and just like I always will, I catch her and crush my lips against hers.

I spin her around as she starts giggling against my mouth. Hearing the commotion Jen and Weston walk over to us. I set Elli down and she all but screams "We're getting married!"

Weston claps me on the back and Jen squeals. Everything I never knew I wanted is standing right there, surrounded by our best friends. It feels so right.

Weston seems to be doing better and has been attending meetings to begin to sort through his PTSD. He was also able to get out of the Corps and is taking it day by day figuring out what he wants to do. I know it's a long road but he knows now that my girl and I are here for him every step of the way. He even took it one step further and contacted his little brother, hoping that reaching out to his only family might help him make even more progress.

The noise of Elli and Jen loudly discussing wedding details is suddenly dwarfed by the deafening sound of a Harley coming down the street and stopping in the front of the house. Jen raises her eyebrows at Elli and I, while Weston's posture snaps stiffly by the grill. My sweet girl comes to me and gives me a quick kiss then leaves to go answer the front door.

I look back at Weston and I can tell he's nervous, this reunion is a long time coming for sure. It won't be easy, but like I said, at least he has us to support him.

When my fiancé returns, she's followed by a tall shadow, thick black beard covering most of his face, dark tattoos winding up his arms and sunglasses shading his eyes. Weston walks over and holds out his hand to his brother. "Sterling, been a long fucking time brother." Sterling nods and shakes Weston's outstretched hand. Elli melts into my side and I kiss the top of her head, happy to stand back and let these two get reacquainted.

Jen pipes up from behind us. "So who ordered the sex on a stick?"

The End

PTSD is not a light subject, and many people suffer from its effects everyday. If you or someone you know is suffering, I hope you will find some of these resources helpful.

http://www.22kill.com/veterans-in-need/

https://www.ptsd.va.gov

http://www.operationwearehere.com/PTSD.html

Acknowledgements

A Million Thank You's

First I want to start out by recognizing and showing my appreciation for all of our Nation's Active Duty and Veteran soldiers. Without you and your sacrifices I wouldn't have the opportunities that I have been blessed with. I wish there were a gesture big enough to show how very appreciated you are, but I guess I can start here.

To my John, thank you so much for letting me write all this down. It was a crazy long ride and as much as you hate reading, you let me read and reread and tweak Quicksand until it was something we were both proud of. Every time I wanted to stop you gently nudged me to keep going, I hope I will always be a nudge for you too. I love you.

To my Twin, Janellie you are my creative outlet and possibly love Raid and Elli more than I do. You watched them go from an idea in the back of mind to the forefront of both of our lives. I love you for always being there cheering me on and making me believe I could actually do it.

To my Britney, girl we actually did it! Your encouragement and excitement made me want to publish just so we could squeal about it. Thank you for always supporting me.

To my rock, Jordan. I don't know where you were all my life but you seriously came to me when I needed you most and I truly believe you are an angel. Thank you for being my book buddy, my release partner and for sharing in this crazy amazing thing we both did.

To the Ace in my back pocket, Kate babe, how did I ever survive without you? I have never known someone as kind and selfless as you and I really owe this entire book to you. Without your unending love and kindness Raid and Elli would just be mine forever. Because of you, they can be free to be everyone else's. I love your heart, I love your mind. I just love you.

To Ellie, the real MVP. You took a chance on a newbie, you made me cry with your comments and you made Quicksand actually make sense. Thank you for being the most badass editor in the biz, I really adore you.

To my incredible parents. Mom, you made me want to make something of myself. You gave me every bit of your determination and grit which carried me this far and will always take me places. You are who I want to be when I grow up because you never give up, you never give in and you always keep going. I love you always. Dad, you always knew I had a writer's soul and here we are, you never once let me forget to believe in the power my words have and you are always cheering me on and telling me I can. I can and I did. I love you forever.

Lastly and most importantly, to all of the readers that took a chance on Raid and Elli. Thank you from the bottom of my heart. I hope you loved them as much as I do, it feels so weird to know that once you've reached this point you will have actually read something I wrote... Yay!

Feel free to stalk me at:
Facebook: www.facebook.com/dyllanjerikson
Instagram: @dyllanjerikson
Twitter: Dyllan_Erikson
Snapchat: Dyllanjennette
Email: authordjerikson@gmail.com

About the Author

Dyllan J. Erikson is a Pacific Northwest Native who loves to motor around the backroads of Oregon in her Mini Cooper. When she isn't writing you can normally find her either watching reruns of *CSI* or reading a new book.